Coast Growers

John Gleeson

RendezVous Crime

Cover design: Vasiliki Lenis / Emma Dolan

LE CONSEIL DES ARTS
DU CANADA
DEPUIS 1957

THE CANADA COUNCIL
FOR THE ARTS
SINCE 1957

Canadä

We acknowledge the support of the Canada Council for the Arts
for our publishing program.

We acknowledge the financial support of the Government of Canada through the
Book Publishing Industry Development Program for our publishing activities.

RendezVous Crime
an imprint of Napoleon & Company
Toronto, Ontario, Canada
www.napoleonandcompany.com

Printed in Canada

12 11 10 09 08   5 4 3 2 1

Library and Archives Canada Cataloguing in Publication

Gleeson, John, 1959-
        Coast growers / John Gleeson.

ISBN 978-1-894917-67-4

        I. Title.
PS8613.L43C62 2008   C813'.6   C2008-905623-X

For Anne,
who read the books too

I: The Hanged Man

One

Accessible from the Lower Mainland only by a forty-minute ferry ride across Howe Sound, the Witka Peninsula is a pocket of earthly paradise lying between Vancouver and the dismal clear-cut pulp and paper country to the north. Witka City, joined at the hip to its namesake native reserve, is the commercial hub, but most of the sixty thousand year-round residents live on rural lots, where lush rainforest gives way to sloping lawns, terraced gardens and orchard groves dating back more than a century. Glacier-fed creeks bless the inhabitants with superb drinking water and spellbinding vistas deep into the mountains.

Locals simply call it the Coast. The luckiest of the blessed live along the thirty-odd miles of shoreline in homes facing a postcard view of Valhalla: the Strait of Georgia backed by Vancouver Island, undulant in the mystical distance, with Gabriola, Valdez and Galliano islands curled at the base of the leviathan.

I was one of the lucky ones. My place was on the water, though many of my neighbours wished a good squall would knock it off the cliff and take it far out to sea. Big money had come to the Coast, and next to the tongue and groove tri-levels and solarplex A-frames, my little four-room fishing shack was clearly out of sync and out of line. To me it was vintage Coast—a remnant of the forties and fifties, when the peninsula was a summer playground for Vancouver's comfortable working class. But to Anderson the surgeon, Chapman the British engineer, Popowich the retired canola farmer from Medicine Hat, even Price the old Vietnam War draft dodger—to them, my place was a drag on property values, and I was the wrecker of the showroom view.

There were some friendly exceptions, however, and George (Jake) Jacobson, twice elected Member of Parliament for the federal constituency of Witka, was one of them. Jake had grown up on the Coast and seemed to appreciate the derelict integrity of my old-fashioned digs. Once he had even remarked that my cabin was the correct character and scale for its lot, which he called the prettiest in the vicinity, owing to the abundance of fruit trees: pear, apple, cherry and plum. Jake also remembered me from my city columnist days at the *Vancouver Star*. As a politician with one foot in Witka and the other in Ottawa, Jake saw me as someone who could understand his often conflicted position on the thorny issues of the day. Someone he could talk to.

I was chopping wood out back when Jake came to visit that Saturday in early August. Though well up in his fifties, Jake had retained the pleasantly pugnacious look of a younger man who didn't believe half of what he heard but found just about all of it funny. He claimed the extra weight he'd put on after entering public life had made him "glad-handier" and inhibited wrinkles.

The usual tucked-in grin was absent as he neared the woodpile. "Catch the radio, chum?" he said.

"Something bad happened?"

"Afraid so. Your old boss passed away."

"Sloan?"

He nodded gloomily.

"How?"

"Radio just said his body was found this morning on Settlers Road. Foul play not suspected. They would've said if it was a car accident, wouldn't they?"

"Must be medical. He was wiry but a worrier. Probably heart. I'll make a call."

In the kitchen, I dialed the home number of Rita Champion-Davis, editor of the *Coast Chronicle*.

"Rita there?" I asked the man's voice.

"And you're?"

"Hi, Bob. It's Pat Ross."

Rita, an Aussie, came to the phone sniffling. "Hello, Pat. Guess you heard the news. Isn't it awful?"

"What the hell happened?"

"Looks like suicide."

"Suicide?"

Jake was standing beside me. When he heard the word, he closed his eyes and scowled.

Rita went on. "He was spotted just after sunrise by an old lady out walking her dog. Suspended from a tree limb."

"No!"

"I know. None of us can believe it."

"I heard it was on Settlers Road. How close to Ian's place?"

"Same general area, further toward the water."

"Did he leave a note?"

"Apparently he did. They gave it to Jan. She's been with the RCMP and the coroner's people all day, poor dear."

"Have you talked to her?"

"Just briefly. She wants us to put out a special tribute edition Tuesday. She got quite upset with me when I asked about Albert's note. Doesn't want to go near cause of death."

Rita sighed, and I could almost see her blowing the dyed blonde strands from her chunky face. "She's the boss now."

"Did you see it coming, Rita? Had Albert been acting strangely?"

"He didn't seem particularly morose to me—maybe a little more into himself than usual. Who's to say with these dreadful things?"

I told her to take care.

"Strung himself up," I said to Jake. I poured coffee, and we sat at the table.

He was shaking his head. "That was the editor you were talking to, Ms Champion-Davis?"

"Titular," I said. "Albert was always calling the shots. After he got into municipal politics, he removed editor from his title, but it was for appearance's sake. Rita was his whipping dog, actually, but she sounds worried about Jan taking over."

"Mrs. Sloan? But she's been working at the paper for years."

"Ad seller, ostensibly. She only worked when the spirit moved her, which wasn't that often. I always liked Jan—she's a beautiful woman, vibrant—but she wasn't a favourite with the staff."

We were quiet for a while.

"Tough on the family," Jake said.

"You bet. Damn cruel."

"I know he was one ornery socialist, but he beat the booze, everyone knows that. Must have suffered from depression. Maybe money troubles too."

"Both, probably. The business never paid enough, at least from what I saw, and his mood was lousy after he lost his bid for mayor. I hadn't talked to him, though, in the last four months. Should've been content with his seat on council, not reached for the brass ring."

"Still, he didn't strike me as the type."

"No. He was a scrapper."

After a long, melancholy pause, Jake tittered. "He raked me pretty good a couple times on his op-ed page. I remember one time—oh, he gave it to me good. I wasn't taking a tough enough stand against them damn Yanks over softwood."

"Oh, yeah. I remember reading that."

"So the day after the paper came out, we ran into each other in the bank. I was flying down to New York that night for that UN plenary session on security I told you about. This was last fall, I believe—right, November. Anyway, I'd just converted must have been five hundred bucks into U.S. currency for my stay in New York. Albert's waiting in line, and he sees me, and I guess he figures I must have been pretty teed off about the editorial. I glared at him a couple times, to make sure he knew I was. Then, when I was done with the teller, I made a beeline straight for him, got right up in his face." He laughed. "You should've seen him, he didn't know what was coming. But instead of blasting him, I fanned the greenbacks under his nose, and I whispered, 'Just here to collect the weekly payoff.' Then I showed him some teeth. His face went through quite a sea change—from fright to delight. Never saw the man laugh so hard."

Jake smiled widely and shook his head at the memory. "No, all in all, he was pretty easy on me in print. Considering my stripes."

"You were too far away. Ottawa wasn't really on his map. He liked killing his meat in his own backyard."

"True enough. Tell you one thing, pardner. He sure enjoyed what you did for him, the short time you did it. I sat with him at a chamber breakfast back in February, and when he found out you and I were neighbours, he couldn't stop saying nice things about your work. Told everyone at the table that he wanted you to be his next editor. Said the two of you would straighten a few things out around here."

"Yeah, unfortunately, he broadcast that wish at every other weekly staff meeting, usually after taking a strip off Rita for bungling an easy job. He'd read bits of my stories out loud and tell her to listen and learn. Created some really ugly feelings in the newsroom."

"I can imagine it would."

"One of the reasons I left—I never told you this—was because when Albert and Jan went away for a couple weeks in April, Rita tried to use some muscle on me. Send me out to Boy Scout jamborees with a camera. I didn't bargain for that, and I didn't stick around to take it. But I also had some problems with Albert's fast and loose approach to laying low the enemy. When he smelled blood, man was he vicious."

"Look at Jerome Charlie," said Jake.

"He assassinated the guy. But Albert treated me well, I'll give him that. We used to do breakfast and had some good talks, good laughs. Yeah." I sat there brooding for a while. "Maybe I shouldn't have quit on him."

"Don't do that." Jake got up and stretched. Then in a familiar gesture, usually reserved for the capital antics of corrupt Liberals or Quebec separatists, (Jake was a Conservative), he stomped a foot and shot a grimace at the ceiling. "Damn!" he said. He placed a friendly hand on my shoulder. "Listen, pardner. Come over later, and we'll split that beer again."

"I'll pop by."

He sauntered back to his house, crossing the surgeon's manicured lawn, giving his head a shake a few times in mute bewilderment at the facts as we knew them.

That was Saturday.

Two

Just before ten o'clock Sunday night, headlights raked the cabin walls, and a tall woman walked shakily down the path to my door. It was Jan Sloan. Her thick black hair was pulled back tight; her brown eyes were huge and imploring and looked like they contained unstable elements.

"Can I talk to you inside?" she said.

She sat down in my green plush rocking chair. Her face was drawn and chapped. I told her I was sorry about Albert. She said thanks and lit a cigarette. She had been in the cabin once before, visiting with her late husband, and I had made Fry's Cocoa for all of us, warming the milk on the Baby Bear wood stove. This time, I brought her an ashtray and opened a window to let out the smoke.

Jan was about forty, which made her more than fifteen years younger than Albert and a couple of years younger than me. She had a striking mug—small, elegant features contrasting with a large, bold mouth. Despite the age gap, the grief that seemed to be searching for a way out of her eyes was undoubtedly real. She had been married to Albert for nine years, but they often carried on like newlyweds, smooching and clowning around the office. Albert was originally from the north of England and was one of those bony-faced charmers with the sergeant-major bristles, resonant deep voice and sparkling baby blues. More than once, his attitude toward Jan had reminded me of John cavorting with Yoko.

"I came here," she said, "because Albert always had a great

deal of respect for you. When you were at the paper, it was like we were winning for once. You were one guy he really trusted and admired."

"I appreciate that, Jan, but I'm not interested in going back."

"I wasn't going to ask you to. Although if you wanted Rita's job, you would have it in a second."

"I don't."

"Fine. That's not why I'm here." Chin held up, she took a long drag and crossed her fine legs. Outside the open window, the fore and aft lights of a tugboat beamed across the water, inching southeast toward the mainland, three lighted barges in distant tow. At that moment, I envied the crew.

"I want you to do something for me. Hear me out anyway."

"Sure."

"This might seem self-serving, but I don't believe Albert took his own life. Pat, I'm positive that he didn't."

"What do the police say?"

She wrinkled her nose in contempt. "They think I'm off my rocker. He left a note. The coroner signed off. Case closed."

"They decided pretty quick."

"I begged them to investigate further. They just looked at me. They don't give a damn. They're so smug—and so dumb. They didn't even treat it as a possible crime scene. Albert's body was removed right away, and the gawkers were trampling the area before I got there."

"What did the note say?"

"Here." She used the same shaking hand that held her cigarette to reach into her purse, knocking ashes all over. The note was on a half page of regular printing paper, torn cleanly at the bottom and folded twice. The long, diagonal scrawl was unmistakable.

I'm sorry about this. No harm is intended to anyone.
There is simply no choice in the matter.
Albert Sloan

"It could mean anything," she said, but there was a question in her eyes.

I reserved comment. "Where did they find it?"

"In his pocket. His coat pocket."

"How did he get to Settlers Road?"

Jan almost lunged at me. "That's one question they can't answer. He didn't drive there, and it's more than a six-mile walk. Even at two in the morning, someone would've spotted him walking along the road with a coil of rope in his hand."

"He could have taken the beach. The tide was out far enough to make it around."

"That's what they're saying, the Mounties. Of course, there was fresh sand on his runners. He walked on the beach every day."

"What do you think happened?"

"That's just it. I don't know. All I know is that he wasn't the least bit suicidal. He's never been suicidal. You knew him. Do you think he was?"

"He didn't seem to be. I didn't know him as well as you did, obviously."

"No. No one was closer to Albert than me, and I'm telling you that man did not have it in him to take his own life. Sure, he was dogging it for a while after losing the election; it was a heavy blow. He was just getting comfortable in politics, and then the rug got pulled out from under him. The campaign drained his energy and our bank account. But that was almost six months ago. If you'd seen him, Pat, especially in the last few weeks, you'd know that he had gotten way past that. He was really upbeat. He had been doing research on a story that he thought would make some big waves. He was chipper. All summer we've been sailing, swimming on the beach, working in the garden. Making love. He's been in great spirits. And then what happens? Suddenly he turns around and *hangs* himself? I don't think so."

"What was the story he was working on?"

"Wouldn't tell me."

"Nothing?"

She shook her head. "Kept it to himself. You know Albert. Didn't want to jinx it. Didn't want to let the genie out of the bottle."

"Did he leave notes behind?"

"If he did, I can't find them. But I can tell you this; he really got onto it after Virgil Wood died last month."

"The poet? He was in his nineties, wasn't he?"

"But he was lucid to the end. And Albert spent a lot of time with him in the hospital those last days. He has some of Virgil's papers in the study. You can look at them if you want."

I'd read some of Wood's published poetry and his animal stories and had no desire to read more. He was an interesting character, though; he'd landed on the Coast during the Great Depression, when the beaches had been like a giant shantytown, littered with tin shacks and lean-tos, and he'd never left. One of the ancient ones.

"Jan, were there any medical or money problems?"

"No, nothing like that. Albert was fit, never took meds in his life, and we have lots of equity. Business was about the same as it's always been. Not easy, but we could always make payroll."

"When did you last see him?"

"Friday night. I went to bed before midnight. He was in the study working. I got the call around seven thirty the next morning. Yesterday. Oh, and I found this at the office." She hauled a black day journal out of her purse. "He didn't usually use it, but Friday—here, look—he wrote down these entries. People he was going to see."

The list started at noon and ended at five p.m., with an extra hour allowed between the last two entries.

12:00 Jerome C.
1:00 L. Loved.
2:00 R. Barlow
3:00 Joe R.

5:00 Sayonara Jan

The last entry was more conclusive than the suicide note, I thought, but I didn't say it.

"I'll tell you what I know," Jan said, leaning over, almost maniacally helpful, "because I've talked to these guys. 'Jerome C.,' that's Chief Jerome Charlie, or ex-chief. He says Albert went to his house to pitch an interview—something really candid about the self-government signing ceremony this weekend and about losing the last band election. In that sense, they were both standing in the same moccasins, but that's not how Jerome saw it. He's never forgiven Albert.

"'L. Loved.' That's Lars Lovedahl, of course. He says Albert went to the Venture-West offices to yell at him about the U Catch 'Em pens, that stupid tourist display they set up in the harbour. Albert was furious about those pens going in; who isn't?

"Roy Barlow says he and Albert were talking about a special advertorial section on the mall. 'Joe R.'—I don't know who he is. And I'm not sure what he meant by writing 'Sayonara Jan.'"

Doubt and pain flooded her face. I tried to keep her talking.

"Did he tell you about any of these meetings later in the day?"

"No, but I hardly saw him Friday. I went to the city and came back on the eight o'clock boat. He was in the study when I got home. I showed him a few of the things I bought—clothes and books—but he was preoccupied with work, and I left him alone. What I would do now to do it again. Just *talk* to him."

She gave in at last and cried, hard. I let her be for a while, then put an arm around her and locked a grip on her heaving shoulder.

I had no words.

"I know he was down after losing the election," she sobbed, "but all his old strength and confidence had come back. He was himself again. He loved his life, and we had a *good* marriage."

She stopped crying abruptly, and her face grew firmly focused and mean. "And what about that Ian J. Cameron?

"What about Ian?"

"Come on. He lives just down the road from where Albert's body was found. He's about to leave the province. Everywhere he went, he bad-mouthed Albert. He's a venomous spider, and if he had a chance to do it, he would do it."

She wiped her eyes with a Kleenex, gaining strength and clarity from her anger. "As soon as I heard where it was," she said, "I thought of Ian."

"So what do you want me to do, Jan?"

"I just want you to look into it. You're a digger. You know the principals. You know the place. Just do some digging. I'll put you back on salary, and let's see what you can turn up."

I said I would. She took my right hand in both of hers and gave me a wounded smile. "That's the best news I've had in two days."

"There hasn't been much competition."

Her second smile was nicer. "You're terrible."

I walked with her up the slope to her car. She declined my offer to drive her home. She said Albert's two grown sons from his first marriage were staying at the house, just stunned by the whole thing, naturally. His aged father was flying in from England; other relatives were coming; the funeral was Friday.

She was a strong woman, I thought, as she spun the car around on the gravel parking-pad and jolted it up the long tree-shrouded driveway to Beach Road.

I figured I'd give it a few days, maybe a week. Let her get past the funeral.

Three

T he Mountie smirked. "I didn't think you would fall for that poor widow's weeping, Pat. But I guess when an available, attractive woman is involved, all bets are off."

Staff-Sgt. Tom Brennan laughed at his worldly brilliance. Brennan had the well-scrubbed, slightly brutal baby face that so many Mounties and military men acquire in early middle age. I had never covered crime beats for the *Chronicle,* but I had dredged up a couple of old unsolveds and run into the usual roadblocks of holdback evidence and zero access to lead investigators. Brennan spoke for everyone in the Witka detachment, but at least he would sit you down in his office and tell you with informal frankness that he wasn't going to tell you anything. And you could quote him on that.

"So you don't see any evidence at all in Sloan's death that could point to homicide?"

"Not a thing. And the more the lady argues, the less doubt we have. I'm talking to you as a family representative, not a reporter, right?"

"I'm not writing anything down."

"Keep it that way. I won't pull any punches. The man had enemies, no question about it. Some go all the way back to the late sixties, when he came here as a young high school teacher. You probably heard the story. How he got fired for extolling the virtues of sex and drugs to fifteen-year-olds in a classroom setting. But there was a bit more to it. There was a stupid little episode involving him sneaking some boys into a strip joint on the highway. And unofficially, I think there were some virgins defiled as well. His feud with the Barlow family goes back to then. Roy's older brother, now deceased, was chairman of the school board that fired him. But lots of people in the community had it in for Sloan after that. Virgins have families, you know. Some even get husbands."

"It's a wonder he didn't set sail."

"Not this sailor. Next thing he does, he gets close to old Mrs. McCracken, and before she kicks off she basically gives him that newspaper, him and his hippie friends. Hear that one?"

"Just what I heard from Albert. That he was living on the beach without a care in the world, except that he was recovering from the bottle, and the widow McCracken came down there one day and offered him the *Chronicle*. She wanted him to use it to save the environment."

"Her family felt he did a number on the old gal. Fought it through the courts but lost."

"He didn't mention that."

"Oh, and then it didn't take him long to buy out the partners—there were three of them—but it's common knowledge that they all believe he cheated them. And they're all still here; I think two are living on welfare."

Brennan started using a toothpick as he ran down the list of fresher enemies.

"You've got the politicians and bureaucrats Sloan went after over the years, quite a few of them losing their jobs or offices due to his targeted attacks. And you know how personal he would get. Then there are the dozens, if not hundreds, of disgruntled former employees—of which you are probably one (though we know you were only slumming); numerous businessmen he put out of business; a couple of key industries that he bludgeoned in print on a regular basis and occasionally crippled; the present mayor and all the other people he slandered after he lost the last election.

"So there was motive for an army. This guy was Richard Widmark riding on the Orient Express. There just wasn't a murder, that's all. There was no physical evidence at the scene or in the background to suggest it was anything other than what it looked like: suicide."

"But he wasn't suicidal."

"How do you know that?" Brennan said with a savage glare. "Because his widow says it's so? You heard about the big story he was supposedly working on, but that he didn't bother telling anyone about?"

"Jan mentioned it."

"Yeah, well, I talked to Virgil Wood's family about that. They say it's a load of rubbish. But they do remember Sloan hanging around the last few months, and you know what? They say he was smoking weed on the property and even doing it in the old man's house. No, methinks the drugs caught up with Mr. Sloan. The wife admitted he was a heavy user 'now and then'. I wouldn't be surprised if they were both doing drugs, frankly." He eyed my ten-month growth of hair. "You too, pal."

"No, I just have large ears. Any idea who Joe R. is?"

"Not a clue."

"Did you go through the directory?"

"On a suicide? Hey, we've got grows to bust, outstanding warrants to act on. We talked to the names we could identify from his daybook. It just confirmed that he was erratic and unstable. There's nothing here, Pat."

I got up and shook Tom's hand. "Never heard you talk so freely."

"Makes a difference when you lay down the pen."

"Mind you, I wouldn't rule out writing something about it at some point."

"But you guys don't touch suicides."

"No. If that's what it is."

"Well, that's what it is."

II: Three Players

Four

I drove across town to the reserve. Jerome Charlie's freshly painted bi-level and neat yard lifted his property a couple of notches above the stubbornly squalid norm, but the Witka Nation was raking in the chips.

The band, consisting of fewer than six hundred souls, was collecting mineral and forest royalties worth millions a year; proceeds from a salmon hatchery that supplied all the fish farms on the peninsula and stocked scores of waterways from Howe Sound to Powell River; shares from a gravel excavation business that had shorn off the entire side of a mountain above Dolphin Inlet, incensing the non-natives who'd built their dream homes facing a now-ruined view; and, most recently, moorage fees from a deep-sea pier used regularly by naval vessels but actually built for docking the merchant freighters needed to load the band's gravel for shipment around the Pacific Rim. And all this was coming in on top of the standard patrimony, such as it was, doled out by the fat cats in Ottawa.

Chief and council, meanwhile, were investing the income from jacked-up leases on hundreds of properties bordering the reserve to get into the grocery business and open other retail enterprises. Band members got jobs out of the deal, and competitive pricing ensured established local firms like

Barlow's were bleeding market share.

Most of this was the work of Jerome Charlie, who had been chief for ten years prior to his electoral defeat last spring.

I knocked on his front door and looked seaward. Beyond the windswept grass of the graveyard, breakers were running cobalt blue. A rusted-out freighter was loading gravel from the mile-long chute that led from the base of the denuded mountain.

Jerome opened the door and eyeballed me without interest.

"Can I come in?"

"You're here; you might as well."

Under the vaulted ceiling, the living room was furnished in best black leather and a glut of carved cedar boxes, some as big as coffins, which doubled as lamp stands and coffee or end tables. Chilkat blankets adorned one of the high oak-panel walls; another was decked out in rows of fabulous masks, many of them ancient, each depicting a spirit of the forest, sea or air; a skookum home entertainment unit took up the wall between. For extra comfort on the gold pile carpet, glossy cougar-skin rugs were scattered in front of the flat-screen TV and the big stone fireplace. In the room's furthest corner hung a trophy eagle-feather bonnet, a gift from the Union of British Columbia Indian Chiefs. The great Chief Dan George had once worn it in a movie, I knew, because I'd seen a picture of the presentation in the paper and had read the cutline.

Jerome was medium height and round. He'd been a mill worker for two decades before he'd become chief, and he projected the upright attitude of a man who's had to work for a living and doesn't take crap. He was dressed in a red-check work shirt and baggy Levis, and under his black ball cap his greying hair was cropped short; in appearance, only the giant silver belt buckle—a coiled Haida sea serpent—set him apart from the prototypical blue collar. He was clean-shaven, and his full mouth was set hard and sour. He stood facing me.

"What do you want?" he said.

"I'm doing some checking into Albert Sloan's last movements. I hear he came by Friday to see you. I just wanted to get your impression of him that day and maybe find out what he was here for."

"What's your impression of zero?"

"Pardon?"

"Sloan was a zero. Zero doesn't make an impression."

"I heard he asked you about doing an interview?"

"He asked something. I had nothing to say to him. I have nothing to say about him."

"Jan Sloan finds it impossible to believe that her husband took his own life."

He stepped right up to me and fully bared his upper row of teeth. "You think I might have *offed* the guy?" he said in my face.

"Come on, Jerome. You're scaring me."

"Then you shouldn't be standing in my house."

This guy was hard to talk to, but I gave it a try, putting lots of air around my words. "I know you've got cause to detest Albert Sloan, deeply. To put it plain, he did a smear job on you. Those stories of nepotism on the reserve and your so-called junket program were designed to hurt you, and I'm sure they did. And I told Sloan when he got that hack editor of his to write them that they weren't properly sourced or backed up, they were transparently one-sided, and the editorials he wrote to run with them were way out there. A couple weeks later, I stopped working for the guy—and that wasn't the only reason I walked, but it was one of them. But the man is dead now. Dead. I just want to know what he came to talk about. On the day that he died."

Jerome's brown eyes were bright and hot. But he finally took a breath. "I told his wife already, and I told the cops. He came to ask me about doing an interview on the signing ceremony this weekend. On *how I felt*." He shouted the words. "He wanted my thoughts, and I gave him my thoughts."

"Which were?"

"I told him to get the hell out of Witka Nation and never set foot here again. Or he might never leave."

"How did he react?"

"He left immediately."

"Did he look rattled?"

"I didn't even look at him." He wasn't looking at me either when he said it.

But he surprised me by walking me to my car. As I climbed in, he pointed toward the highway.

"When you drive out, you'll notice the carvers at work in the shed behind the band office. Those twelve faceless poles we put up four years ago have come down. Faces are being carved into them. Witka Nation is getting its identity back. We had to go to the white man and ask for it to be returned. Now that we have it, we have fools in charge who don't understand what it means. The new chief and most of the new council were Sloan's allies. That tells you what fools they are."

Before walking away, he added: "We get enough suicides around here with our young people that Sloan's death counts for nothing. Dog control day makes me sadder."

I slowed down as I passed the carving shed. A jumbo mouth showed near the foot of the pole nearest me, bear teeth bared the way Jerome Charlie's had been. With no eyes or ornamental lines to frame it, it struck me as demonic. I had a sense of why the Witka, tough as they were, used to fear the forest.

Five

On Cowrie Street, I noticed the coffee shops were full of *Star* readers, and the red metal boxes had been emptied of the Monday edition. I went into Hoy's Grocery and picked up a copy. The story was on page 12. Salim Marwari had the byline. Salim and I had come up together on the suburban weeklies. At the *Star,* I was handed the political beats and eventually wrote columns for forward news. Salim stuck with general assignment, specializing in crime and death. He loved lurid sensationalism but had a good heart, whereas Sloan made a show of despising crime news and sensationalism but was widely regarded as heartless. One of those paradoxes.

The story was short. Sudden death—no mention of suicide—had taken a local Witka legend. The story listed Sloan's achievements in print and amateur theatre. The only quote was from the new mayor, a cake decorator at Barlow's. "Certainly not everyone agreed with all his opinions," she said, "but he loved the Coast and was a kind of watchman over it. He'll never be quite replaced."

Not a bad quote.

I crossed Cowrie and entered the storefront offices of Venture-West, which were as slapdash and impersonal as Venture-West itself.

Venture-West was Lars Lovedahl's name for his latest government-funded scheme to promote the salmon farm industry on the Coast. Lovedahl was a Norwegian-born economic development officer who'd been hired by the regional district to goose the local economy. In three years, he had done little for existing businesses; his singular and stellar achievement was establishing the Coast as a major aquaculture centre in North America. The number of fish farms in the area had grown from five to more than fifty under Lovedahl's guiding hand, with a hundred more waiting in the wings. Most of the investment was foreign: Scandinavian mainly, but also British, American and Japanese.

Lovedahl had been riding high until last winter. Then I guess I came along. Quoting renowned marine biologists, including the few B.C. experts who were not directly or indirectly employed by government, my series in the *Chronicle* had exposed the new industry as an economic and environmental disaster in the making. Even industry cheerleaders from Washington State to Iceland conceded that the warm water temperatures in the inner gulf were unsuitable for raising salmon, and that widespread, chronic disease among the stocks was virtually a sure thing. Though Lars denied it, claiming controls were in place to prevent it, the experts were convinced that heavy doses of antibiotics in the feed to fight the contagion, and the diseased stocks themselves, would contaminate the finished product, along with native species and other marine life as feed and fish escaped into the wild. This could eventually have a shattering impact on the commercial and sport fisheries, both foundations of the Witka economy.

The B.C. government and the feds put up their own biologists to refute the claims, arguing that the industry was too new to draw definite conclusions, even though the European and American experiences were more than a decade old and well-documented. Local proponents sank themselves by acknowledging the main reason they wanted to establish Witka as their beachhead was the proximity to the Vancouver market, which also made it ideal to showcase their hardware to potential investors. "So it's a trade-off," one fish farmer naïvely admitted.

Not that the industry was really sunk. Most farms had been granted ninety-nine year leases for the coves and bays they occupied, so they weren't going anywhere. But public opinion on the Coast swerved hard against the industry, and Victoria acceded to demands for a moratorium on new operations. As a Witka City alderman, Sloan sat as a director on the regional board, and he delivered the *coup de grâce* by having Lovedahl fired for negligence in the performance of his duties.

Now Lars was back on a tourism grant. His idea of U Catch 'Em pens in the harbour had flopped badly—who wanted to catch catatonic salmon floating inside a steel cage?—but he had the province's money in hand and had to go through with the scheme until the Labour Day weekend.

The reception room was empty, so I called out.

"Come! Come! I'm in here." Lovedahl was on the phone in the main office, bare except for a metal desk, two chairs, a faux antique globe and a large wall map of the Coast. On it the farms were flagged with pins whose heads were shiny pink salmon.

"I'll just be a minute. I'm on long—" He saw who I was and looked away. Then he came back to life on the phone, speaking in rapid-fire Norwegian, probably negotiating terms for a couple of Gulf Islands.

Lars was a big man, a bearded Viking with shaggy auburn hair, china blue eyes and a neat elfin nose. Intelligent and affable, I had long suspected him of being an evil genius.

He motioned for me to sit down while he stood up and ended his call. Then out came his big hand and his bright buccaneer smile. "My old nemesis," he said warmly.

I had to laugh and say, "How've you been doing?"

He leaned back in his swivel chair, feeling his ample rib cage and gazing around the room judiciously. "It's a big comedown from my old offices, but this was a temporary thing. Served its purpose, helped put a human face on the industry."

"So that was the purpose."

"We have to educate. We're here to stay." He gestured to the wall map. "What you never understood, my friend, is that the wild stocks are dying. Those guys out there are hunting buffalo. Soon we'll be the only game in town, and there'll be a whole world looking to us to feed them."

"We're all in this together."

"Exactly."

"Then I take back everything I've ever written."

He gave me his booming laugh. "What can I do for you today, Pat Ross? Looking for a job? One of the farms could probably use your talents."

"I don't shoot osprey. No, I'm poking around to find out what I can about what happened to Albert Sloan."

Lovedahl raised his eyebrows dramatically. "What happened to him? We all know what happened. He killed himself."

"Not everyone's certain of that."

He shook his head sadly, crimping his lips. "The widow, eh? Poor woman. It must be hard for her to accept. When these things happen, you know, usually there's some serious trouble in the marriage bed."

"Did Albert look seriously troubled when he came in here Friday?"

"He looked the way he always looked. A prancing gamecock. Threatening to blast us out of the water. That's the only side of him I ever saw."

"Threatening to blast the U Catch 'Em thing out of the water?"

"That, and the whole industry. He'd been talking to some of the resort people, said tourist numbers were down—*it's been a wet summer.* But he blamed the farms. The pens were attracting dogfish, discouraging boaters, all the old fears. He sounded off and left."

"Pretty pointless visit."

He nodded, sputtering agreement, eyes lowered.

"What did you say to him?"

He smiled, showing his little King Oscar teeth. "I told him he could talk about it all he wanted, but he had nobody good left to write it."

"Thanks."

"He *was* wired, I'll grant you that. He was never a relaxed person, but this time he was really wired. I thought he might have had a drink in him, but I heard he didn't drink. Was he suicidal? How would I know that? I was floored when I heard what he did. He didn't seem generous enough to please so many enemies at once."

"Were you pleased when you heard?"

"I was an enemy, as everyone knows. He attacked me, tried to ruin me, gloated when he got me fired. Wanted the resolution to read *gross* negligence, but the board wouldn't go that far."

"I remember that."

"Oh, I hated his guts. But when I heard about it, I didn't feel good. I didn't feel broken up or anything, except I did feel bad for his family. They're the ones that have to live with it. I know one thing, though. If it had been me instead of him, Sloan would've been dancing in the streets. No?"

I wasn't going to argue that one.

Six

Roy Barlow had his office in a bland grey four-storey building next to Barlow's Foods, the supermarket anchor for his shopping centre, the largest in Witka. Beyond the drab façade, the interior of the Barlow Enterprises headquarters was appointed to the gills, with the fossil record showing in the polished limestone lobby floor and manta rays skirting around behind reception in a tank bigger than a Natchez Line boxcar. A mini-conservatory at mezzanine level cheered your passage as you were boosted up in the see-through elevator to the boss's office on the top floor.

Barlow was the richest citizen operating on the Coast, owner of reputedly half the city's real estate and a quarter of its businesses. He was a deacon in his church and was often derided by locals as loftily and pompously High Anglican. In my few encounters with him at public functions, Barlow had always struck me as courteous and reserved, albeit a tad prissy. I hadn't detected a real sanctimonious side. His refusal to advertise any of his businesses in the *Chronicle* after Sloan became publisher, however, was universally interpreted as moral condemnation, pure and simple; and though it made Sloan a hero of sorts with some of Barlow's competitors and members of the counterculture set, it ensured the *Chronicle* would never turn a healthy profit.

The animosity, of course, ran both ways. Older *Chronicle* staff spoke of historic near-resolutions to the feud being blown at the eleventh hour, always by Sloan, who couldn't let go of his grudge and cut a deal with "the man".

Deep concern showed in Barlow's pigeon-grey eyes as he led me to a niche overlooking a fine sweep of harbour and the strait. I sat down on a black and red mohair sofa, and he sat facing me in a lemony waved-back chair with some chrome coming out of the arms. He was a funny looking guy. His near-bald head seemed large for his thin frame, and his ears seemed large for his head. He was wearing the same power ensemble—royal blue suit with red tie and gold clip— that the prime minister had worn during his recent visit to Washington. It went nicely, I noticed, with the chair.

He crossed his legs and clasped both hands on his knee, gold band up. "How is Mrs. Sloan doing, Pat, or have you had a chance to talk to her yet?"

"Yeah, she's in rough shape. Taking it very hard."

"It must be an awful weight on her. I spoke to her briefly yesterday—she called me at home asking about a meeting I had with Albert on Friday—and she was so upset. She wasn't taking it well at all."

"She can't believe it was suicide."

"I got a sense of that. I don't know how it could be otherwise. From what I hear, the coroner ruled it suicide, and they're very meticulous, especially nowadays with all the forensic tools at their disposal. Maybe it's a self-defense mechanism. She needs more time before she can fully accept it."

"You might have something there. Nice pictures," I said, needing to change the subject.

Barlow swivelled around and smiled up at the wall behind him. There were half a dozen framed glossies of sharks taken at extremely close range. "It's the one way I indulge myself. Some people smoke, some people drink. I'm an amateur underwater photographer. That one's a great white."

These guys and their great white whales, I thought. Why not put a sign up: *Call me Ahab.* "You sure got close," I said.

"You're down there in a cage. There really isn't much risk at all."

"So you saw Albert that last day."

"He was here, in this office, from about one thirty to two in the afternoon. He showed up early for a two o'clock appointment, and I brought him right in. I told him about some ideas I had for a supplement on the mall that would involve editorial copy on a few initiatives that we're pretty excited about."

"He was receptive?"

"Seemed interested. Maybe a little quiet, but attentive. Albert and I have been over this ground before. I use radio and flyers, but there are things newspapers do best, and competition is getting fiercer, with the band stepping up quite an aggressive pricing war on a variety of retail fronts. I'm looking at protecting my interests. But Albert and I have baggage—had baggage, I guess I should say—and we were moving very slowly."

"What was the baggage about?"

"I would prefer not going there, frankly, Pat. The man is dead. But since I brought it up, there was a time long ago when Albert was a fairly unsavoury character. He said some very abusive things to members of my family. Even after he got his hands on the *Chronicle,* he never conducted himself in a businesslike fashion, not at all, and I simply won't do business with people whose judgment I can't trust."

He shifted thoughtfully, and I could sense that he was now going to pretty things up.

"I think getting into municipal politics worked a positive change in Sloan's outlook. He finally started to see what the world was really about. It's so different when you're sitting in the gallery tossing down brickbats. I noticed, even when he was here the other day, that a lot of the old arrogance was gone. It's just tragic that he would end his life after coming so far."

"Did he ever mention the poet Virgil Wood to you?"

Barlow looked nonplussed. "No. Why would he?"

"Jan says he was quite excited by something he learned from him before Wood's passing. Wood went way back. And, well, your family was here before anyone, except the Witka. Didn't they call the whole area Barlow's Landing for many years?"

"Yes, from the 1880s through to the 1930s. But there were other families, too—the Hamiltons, the Douglases, the Mullens, the McBrides. My great-grandfather just happened to row his boat across first and staked out some sizable claims."

"I see."

"No, Albert didn't talk about past history on Friday. Not ours, and not Witka's. He did seem somewhat distracted, but that's not very unusual for you people. Media types, I mean. Perhaps he left some notes on the subject."

"Jan says she couldn't find them." I yawned. "Sorry. I'd forgotten how tiring it was asking questions to men behind desks. At least our talk was a little more comfy." I got up to go. "Appreciate your time, Roy."

"Any time, Pat." His hand was clammy when we shook. "Back in the writing saddle?"

"No, not for print around here," I said, and I left it at that.

At a natural wood bakery by the harbour, I downed a toasted tomato, cheese and cucumber sandwich then took my coffee mug outside and fed secondhand smoke to the seagulls.

Well, the morning was shot.

III: Sightings

Seven

I drove south along the highway to Settlers Road, pulling into Ian J. Cameron's driveway behind his Nissan Pathfinder, which was mounted on blocks. Ian stepped out of the house to greet me before I made it to the back door. His smile was warm, but behind the big wire-frame glasses cool curiosity showed in his pale blue eyes.

Ian was a well-built, good-looking man in his late thirties, with a high, speckled forehead under thinning sandy hair, a lantern jaw and a large mouth that was frequently set in a roguish grin. He had done some serious bodybuilding in his youth, and though he stood three or four inches under my six feet, he must have had at least forty pounds on my glutted hundred and sixty. As advertising manager at the *Chronicle,* Ian had been permanently disgruntled by the time I had gone to work there late last year, and had quit in the spring, about a month after me.

"You're still here," he said.

"*You're* still here. I thought you were moving the family back to Ontario."

"Before school starts. We're still hoping to unload the house first. And I gotta get this pig"—he pointed to the Pathfinder—"roadworthy."

He lowered his voice and moved closer. "Have to get the

girls away from this freak show. You know Connie, our thirteen-year-old? She has a paper route. If she'd been up an hour earlier Saturday morning, that would've been her discovering that goof hanging from the old apple tree. I call that getting too close to home for comfort."

"Can you show me where it was?"

He considered the question. "I'll just let Tish know."

He stepped back into the house and came out after a few minutes, banging the door. His delinquent look suggested he was acting against the better judgment of a higher authority. The kitchen curtain, I noticed, was being tweaked.

Ian brushed past me. "Let's go," he said.

We walked about a quarter mile down an easy grade toward the sea. He led me to the site. It was a deep lot, unfenced and overgrown, packed with mature apple trees, some nearing full production. He stood by an old giant that grew close to the road.

"Here."

"Fine big tree," I said, patting the trunk. It was one of those pulled-wishbone-shaped beauties, with Atlas arms supporting a dense crown of leaf and upper limbs.

"Natural born hanging tree," Ian said, nodding up at one of the high sturdy boughs.

"I guess." I got a chill looking at a pair of big moss-covered rocks on the ground that could have been jump-off points, I supposed. I was picturing the mechanics of the thing.

"Who owns the lot?"

"Some people in Port Moody. He's an accountant, I think. They haven't built on it yet, obviously, but they'll be out soon to strip the trees and cut the grass. They stay in a camper when they're here."

"Beautiful lot."

"Oh, it's choice. Across the street—" Ian pointed to a big ranch-style bungalow set among towering cedars and hemlocks—"that's where the municipal office was back in the Barlow's Landing days."

"Really? I didn't know that."

"There's plenty you don't know, son. The settlers planted these old fruit trees all over the Coast, but this area is the epicentre. With the mostest and the oldest. This was all part of the original Barlow homestead, which covered about two-thirds of the peninsula. Then, during the war, the settlers' heirs carved up this and the four other major holdings and turned the Coast into cottage country. More money in cottage lots than jam factories. And then those cottage folk have to buy their groceries and their gas and their egg foo yung. Then you need schools for the gas jockeys' kids. Doctors for the teachers. Upscale car dealerships and teak furniture emporiums for the doctors. And behold: Witka is born."

"Look at that," I said. The right side of the trunk had a long gash in it, extending about six inches. Time and weight had almost flattened it, but a layer of dark moss grew out like fur from an old man's ears.

Ian whistled. "Some long ago fool started chopping this mother down. Sanity prevailed, and the tree endured."

We started back. A strong breeze was blowing off the sea, and laughing women were straining against it, pulled along by mammoth protein-rich dogs hungry for the beach. Cars shot by with their pre-school passengers, little faces flying past us with doubtful expressions.

"I saw the goof down here last month."

"Albert?"

"That's him, was him. Yeah, it was about the middle of the month. I was driving Tish to work, and he was standing right where we just stood, looking at self-same hanging tree."

"Really? Did you tell the Mounties that?"

"Oh, they paid a visit. And I told them."

"Did they say anything?"

"Mounties?"

"Right. How did Sloan look?"

"The usual dazed. Looking up—waaaaay up—as the Friendly Giant used to. And I wouldn't swear to it, but I also got the impression that he was wearing that famous wolfish leer of his, but I wouldn't swear."

"Like hell you wouldn't."

"Okay, I did. I cursed him when we passed. I curse him in my sleep, too. You know, I sold his advertising for almost seven years. One day, I was standing in Safeway, closing a quarter-million-dollar account, and you know what? I looked down and I realized I had holes in the soles of my shoes. That ditzy wife of his drew the same salary I did—and what she sold during a week, I sold during a coffee break."

"Remember what he used to say: 'To keep everyone equal—'"

"'Everyone must earn equal keep.'" Ian J. Cameron spat. "What a loser."

Eight

I left Ian's place and drove back to the scene. I door-knocked and got lucky on the fifth house, a blue and white pre-fab dropped on a swampy piece of unevenly sodded ground. A bony old Scot, actually wearing a kilt below a plain white T-shirt, stepped out of the house—a toy dog inside was letting out a mighty yap—and spoke to me on his huge, unfinished, untreated deck that was already decaying at the edges. He looked like he was recovering from yesterday's libations, but his brown eyes appeared intelligent and honest. He had a pencil-thin black moustache, and his hair was also dyed jet black.

I asked him if he'd seen or heard anything that might have had a bearing on Albert Sloan's death.

"You know, I saw that fella here, wandering around over in the apple grove. I was out pulling some weeds, and I noticed him. Knew the face from his column in the paper. There was him and another fella."

"Another fellow?"

"Biker looking, I'd describe him. Tall, tattoos, big arms on him, wee black leather vest, that shambling strut—you know: these boots are made for kicking. Mind you, a lot of them look that way these days. Could just as easily been a psychiatric nurse. Sounds like the poor bugger needed one badly."

"When was this?"

"Oh, let me think. Before Canada Day, I know that," he said, a touch of pride showing in his recollection, though it was probably of a wicked bender. "But not much before. Maybe two, three days. It was the end of June."

"This biker, hair long or short?"

"Short. Almost a crew cut."

"What colour?"

"Light brown, with some grey."

"Beard?"

"Yes, but trimmed neat."

"Age?"

"I'd guess late forties. Hard to tell with all that get-up."

"What did it look like they were doing?"

"Milling around, looking at the property."

"Did you tell this to the RCMP?"

"Probably ought to, eh?"

"You should. You got a pretty good look at the guy."

"But the Sloan fella did himself in, from what they're saying?"

"Who's saying?"

"All the neighbours." He pointed to the house on his right.

"You should still report it."

He looked at me intently and took a man-size breath. "That I will."

* * *

Sloan's house on Beach Road was an old summer cottage that had been extensively remodelled. It was built along a curved stretch where road and sea joined very close. Lush hedgerows lent the property an old country charm and kept all but the red-tiled roof hidden from passing traffic.

Jan answered the door and led me along the hall, not bothering to introduce me to the grieving relatives who had taken over the living room. I caught a glimpse of two sombre young men on the sofa and a very old, weathered and defeated version of Albert, sitting low in a recliner. They were all watching television. I heard women's voices in the kitchen. I followed Jan to the study.

First, I told her about the biker. She said she had no idea who it could be. "Albert knew all kinds of Coast people." I said it meant Albert had been down there at least twice before Friday and asked her to try to remember anything he'd said that could shed light on why.

Jan shook her head. "No, the first I heard of it was when the RCMP told me this morning. They said they'd found a witness, but it didn't change anything in their minds. They won't reopen the investigation. I called a staff meeting today, got everyone together in the composing room, and I put it to them. No one at the paper knows anything about what he was doing there or what he was working on."

I didn't mention the fact that Ian J. Cameron was the witness the RCMP had "found" and was glad she didn't press for details. I figured Jan was behind the Mounties going to Ian's house, and I didn't want to give her more ammo to use against him. But I did tell her about my interviews in town that morning, choosing my words carefully. The truth is, I felt Jerome Charlie's and Lars Lovedahl's stories were very weak; unless Albert had grown senile since I knew him, he would never have faced off with either one armed with so little. Barlow I just didn't get a good feeling from. What I told Jan was that their stories could have holes in them—maybe holes big enough to drive a truck through—but there was nothing definite to go on yet.

She didn't look satisfied with that, but she had to accept it.

She loaded me up with a cardboard box filled with Virgil Wood's writings, most of them in typewritten manuscript, crowning the stack with a videocassette documentary on the poet.

I carried it out to the car and drove home.

Nine

I steamed some rice and was grilling a piece of lingcod when the phone rang.

"Pat, is that you?"

I knew the voice. It was Max Riverton. He was a semi-retired aircraft mechanic who had become unofficial leader of the anti-aquaculture movement on the Coast after a Norwegian company set up its salmon pens outside his picture windows at Dundee Bay. Max used to call me regularly at the *Chronicle*.

"How are you doing, Max? What's up?"

"Lots. Listen, I heard you were in to see Lovedahl today. Are you back in the war?" I didn't answer. Max considered Lovedahl next in line to the devil and always claimed he was a secret investor in several of the farms, including the eyesore at Dundee Bay.

"Because if you are, I've got some very interesting stuff for you. I told it all to Sloan last week but, well, he can't do anything with it now."

"All right. What is it?"

"It's Lovedahl. He's been seen all over Dolphin Inlet with two strange Germans. No one knows who they are or what exactly they're doing here, but they're holding major confabs at the Witka hatchery—they always seem to meet there over the lunch hour. Something is definitely up. There's talk of a serious outbreak."

"Did Sloan tell you he got anything?"

"No, he never called back. Next thing I heard he was dead."

"Well, I'll see what I can find out."

"Watch those bastards."

"I will, Max. Thanks."

After supper, I tackled the Virgil Wood papers. I found nothing of relevance and little of interest in them—some dull animistic Indian fables, a long memoir about growing up on a farm somewhere, notes for what looked like children's stories, reams and reams of nature poetry. Too many plum blossoms and surrendering sunsets for my taste.

The video was a twenty-five minute profile of Wood that had aired almost ten years before on CBC, called *Milk From the Mountains*. It followed him along the beach, where he talked about the Depression-era squatters, with names like Plymouth Jim, the Baptist Kid and Fast Edna. His discovery in the 1960s, with a couple of university profs talking about his original vision and poetic integrity. A short bittersweet segment about his wife, a teacher, who predeceased him. Scenes of Virgil at home, Virgil in a classroom reading to school kids, Virgil walking down Cowrie Street and venturing into New Age clip joints where his books were for sale. Voiceovers with the standard idolatry of native culture and whisperings about ghosts in yonder hills—shrines of the disinherited, he called them. A final reading of verses to shifting wilderness images of the Coast, ending with a view of the sun hanging low over the Strait of Georgia and Virgil intoning: "I close my eyes to see ablaze…your sky of orange."

I tucked it all away and walked over to my neighbour Jake's place for a beer.

Jake's wife Helen was a once-beautiful blonde who still carried herself with a lot of class but now had the sliding jawbone of a chronic tippler. She asked if that was Jan Sloan she'd seen on my porch the night before. So they wouldn't get any wrong ideas, I told them what Jan's visit was about, asking them to keep it strictly under their hats. They were quite tickled to hear that I was looking into Albert's death.

"Solve the mystery and win the widow," Helen quipped. "And don't worry about us talking. Like Jake says, since he's been in Ottawa, he's heard so many state secrets that he would be a security risk if he remembered half of them."

"Good for Mrs. Sloan," Jake said. "Who knows, she could be right. But good for her even if she's not. She's got some gumption. And loyalty."

Jake looked like he had been keeping up with Helen in the sauce department, but assumed a sober expression when I told him about the Max Riverton call. He said he would contact the federal fisheries people and ask them to look into it.

"So did Albert know about this?" Jake said.

"He did."

"And our friend Mr. Lovedahl knew that he knew?"

"I'd bet money that's why Sloan visited Lars on Friday, though Lars hasn't told anyone that."

Jake gave it some dark thought, then seemed to discard the implications. "That would be a real stretch, pardner."

Jake spilled out a shoebox two-thirds filled with old comics. The selection was heavy with westerns, most of them sporting amazing decayed Joe Maneely dark pulp covers.

The way Jake explained it half-seriously one time, in the same way America went wrong after Kennedy was killed, comics went wrong after Joe Maneely fell under a New York commuter train in 1958. Only thirty-two, he had been Stan Lee's house artist at Atlas, king of the westerns and master of all genres. Jack Kirby got the job and went on to flood comics with monsters then impossibly built superheroes. The age of reason had left.

I got a kick out of Jake's biases, but I couldn't dispute the immense talent of Joe Maneely. You could almost smell the piney woods coming off some of those covers, his figures and scenes were pointed with life, the frontier characters looked authentic, as did the backdrops and gear. Beautiful brush and pen lines like Steve Ditko's Spider-Man at peak, and they say Joe was fast.

Joe probably drew more western heroes than any artist in comics. Throw out a name and add "kid" and you've got a Maneely western hero. Western Kid, Ringo Kid, Outlaw Kid, Apache Kid, Rawhide Kid, Two-Gun Kid, Kid Colt, Texas Kid, Arizona Kid and Matt Slade Gunfighter, aka Kid Slade. And those were just the kids with their own titles. Joe also drew one-shots for anthology series like *Gunsmoke Western* and *Cowboy Action*, tossing off the Pecos Kid, the Prairie Kid, the Abilene Kid, the Hair-Trigger Kid, even the Yahoo Kid. Plus he did Wyatt Earp, the Gunhawk, and the title that made his reputation in 1950, Black Rider.

I sat back and admired a couple of Maneely *Ringo Kid* yarns and a pre-code *Texas Kid*. The pre-code westerns have such childishly frequent fatal shootings.

On the coffee table, Jake lined up some pastel Carmine Infantino *Mystery in Space* covers—figures, devices, alien skylines imbued with swinging Telstar-era innocence.

"Striking," I said.

"Elegant, as befits the Kennedy years."

As we flipped pages, we talked about the Kennedy years, then about Kennedy.

"One thing we do know," I said, "is Northwoods didn't happen on Kennedy's watch."

"Northwoods. Was that a Gladio?"

I shut *Texas Kid*. "No, Northwoods was before Gladio went operational, at least with strategy of tension. Gladio was set up for Europe, but Northwoods was a homegrown plot, it had all the generals onside, and part of the plan was to launch terrorist attacks against random Americans in Miami, and I think D.C., blame Cuba and invade."

"This was when?"

"Sixty-two."

"Really. And Kennedy snuffed it?"

"They don't have it documented that the plan got to Kennedy. It's a stretch that it didn't; the Joint Chiefs had all signed on. What we do know for sure is it didn't happen."

"But Gladio happened. What was it, a NATO thing? See, I count on you for all my Mother Jones Earth News, pardner."

"You remember all those media reports back in the seventies about bombings in Italy? Big public places like train stations, starting with the Piazza Fontana in 1969. Blamed on Red Brigades or some left-wing extremists. Lot of innocent people were killed, policemen were murdered, politicians kidnapped and murdered."

"Of course. It was all over the news."

"Right. They went operational in other countries too. Germany, Turkey, I think Belgium. Always blamed on Red Brigade type groups. You'd picture these ruthless young German militant hippie nihilist types, right?"

"Right."

"The type you get in all the movies."

"Right. But it turned out..."

"It turned out they were the opposite. Far right fascist types, organized and supposedly set up under NATO by the CIA after the Second World War. Yeah. Trained with Green Berets and British Special Air Service. They were called stay-behind armies, and their original purpose was to fight against a possible Soviet invasion of Europe."

"But which never happened."

"Right. So, in 1969—and remember, this is the version in some academic circles; not everyone agrees, and a U.S. government bulletin, put out not that long ago, categorically denies U.S. involvement in any of the terrorist activities; the bulletin also claims the top researchers who support the CIA-sponsored theory have cited a known Soviet forgery many times and were duped into believing it was from a U.S. intelligence manual—but in 1969, regardless of U.S. involvement, some of these cells started to employ a concept called the strategy of tension. Carry out acts of terror against your people, blame the appointed enemy (up to and including planting evidence) and hide behind state protection because it's all for the state. There was considerable worry in those days that the public was drifting too far to the left. So a violent remedy was applied. They killed a lot of people."

"How did it finally get out?"

"Gladio was blown, I believe, in 1984 when one of the bombers started talking at his trial. There were big European Union statements condemning the U.S. around 1990, and Italian Senate hearings in 2000, both times unfortunately when Americans were about to head to war in the Middle East, so we didn't hear much about it."

"You're not saying there's a connection?"

We laughed.

"In the end, NATO admitted ownership of Gladio and said nothing else. The U.S. admits it was involved but deny they had anything to do with any rogue operations."

"Seems plausible," Jake said, then smiled.

"Seems far-fetched to me, considering Gladio went on the rampage for more than fifteen years, and NATO, which means the Pentagon, was master during that whole span of time. But deny they did."

"And deny they will. You know, pardner. The public isn't all as innocent as you make out. You'd be surprised how many people support these things. Maybe not consciously, but they know there's a connection between their comfort, their job, their safety and a lot of nasty things that happen in the world to people who least deserve it. And they can live with that."

"Sure, but the basic track to me is that people are too generally sane to comprehend a psychopath, and that's what psychopaths count on. But I see it too. Well just look at what came out last year with the JFK shooting. E. Howard Hunt's deathbed confession: LBJ ordered it, and four CIA agents involved were named. Some of it—the road trip to Dallas—had come out before in a libel suit trial, when a woman ex-agent gave testimony. But this was Hunt, who had been denying everything all along. Finally, near death, he was revealing something of the truth to his son. But my point: remember when everyone was talking about that obnoxious Oliver Stone movie?"

"Of course."

"Then along comes something real, the most explosive new evidence I'd say since the Warren Commission, because Hunt was a major player—"

"Oh, he was that." Jake's head nodded briskly.

"Not a bit of interest. *Rolling Stone* buries the lead, and except for one paper in Los Angeles, the media ignores it. Looks like the JFK story crossed the line into pure entertainment. Talk about turning history into myth."

"I guess they're waiting for the movie, pardner."

I nodded, finished my beer, declined another, declined something stronger, declined a game of Scrabble, and went home.

I finally got to sleep. I dreamt my children needed me.

Ten

The water was still heating on the Baby Bear stove when Irving Walters paid a visit the next morning. "Saw your chimney," he said, "so I brought you over these." He was holding an upside-down bouquet of lightly filled shopping bags in his huge gnarled hand.

Irving was more than a hundred years old, a hunched little Englishman who had retired to the Coast almost forty years earlier, after selling his dairy spread in Alberta. He had a wife named Minnie who was much younger than him, but Minnie was ill and stayed mostly indoors. Irving, on the other hand, was a going concern, maintaining his large property, a garden, a greenhouse and a visiting regimen that exasperated some of the neighbours, which he found amusing. His mother had signed a temperance pledge for him in 1902, when he was an infant, and he had never taken a drink in his life. He was proud of that. He got into the First World War as a bugle boy and witnessed the horrors of the trenches first-hand—lads and horses blown to bits. He blamed capitalism and man's innate stupidity, considered all wars evil, and regarded all celebrations or commemorations of war, including Remembrance Day, as vile rituals that served only to perpetuate the madness.

His drooping eyes could be an awful, watery mess, sending discharges like gobs of vitreous humour streaking down around his bulbous nose, but otherwise he was remarkably intact for his age.

"Like to come in, have a coffee or a cup of tea?"

"No, I've had my two strong cups, thank you. Just dropping this off, making the rounds." The plastic grocery bags contained two small succulent heads of butter lettuce and, underneath them, an earthy dozen of new potatoes. "First of the season," he smiled, standing on the porch with almost schoolboy expectancy. Irving lived one house over from Jake. The two friendly exceptions. "So they did in that socialist fellow you worked for. It doesn't seem so extraordinary."

"What do you mean, 'they' did him in, Irving?"

He chuckled. "They, the world. Got to him, got him back. He made waves and went under."

"Ah."

"He seemed to have a lot of crackling vitality in him, but I guess you can't really judge a man by his writing."

"No, I guess not. As one American writer wrote, writing is a way for madmen to appear sane."

Irving brayed at the Vonnegut line. "Wrote that, did he? Quite so, I suppose, although I daresay you can still judge the grade of lunatic from his writing. This Sloan had a very pretty wife, didn't he?"

I nodded.

"Kind of a Spanish type," Irving said. "I saw them together in the mall one time. A real Dona Maria, she was. I'd go on experimental life support for an indefinite duration, let them stick tubes in my brain and everything, if I could have her coming around ten minutes a day for tea and biscuits. I'd even let them refrigerate my withered carcass if there was a chance of climbing under a warm blanket with her after they thaw me out. Maybe they'd develop the technology to rebuild me so she wouldn't have to wear a mask."

The old soldier smiled dreamily under the spell of his scientific romance, then glanced over toward his house, probably remembering sick Minnie holed up inside.

"Oh well, more's the pity that they got him in the end. Have to be careful," he said, waving goodbye.

As he crossed the yard, a bald eagle lifted off from the tip of a giant spruce. Irving had company on his rounds.

I ate my wild oats, realizing I had been warned twice in the last twelve hours.

Eleven

I walked to Seaview Market, a general store and snack bar at the south end of Beach Road. Sally was leaning on the snack bar counter, reading the *Chronicle.* I picked up a copy and sat down on a stool across from her. Sally was a big, trim, handsome lass in her late twenties who would be a natural first-round pick for any women's softball team. Sally owned and operated Seaview with her firefighter husband. It was a handy setup, because the fire hall was next door. At the moment she was deep in the paper.

"Wanna coffee?"

"I guess I can handle one more, but no hurry."

Sally poured, speaking quickly, her face animated. "I didn't realize he was in so many plays. He even played King Lear." Then she was back in the paper.

I went through the Albert Sloan tribute edition. They did do a nice job. Stories and photo spreads on Albert the environmental activist, Albert the opinion maker, Albert the philanthropist, Albert the public office holder, Albert the community builder, Albert the sailor and beachcomber, Albert the dean of local amateur theatre. He was all these things and more.

Rita wrote a gushing piece about being mentored by the master, with anecdotes. Jan did something more honest about Sloan's deep attachment to the Coast and his dream of retiring one day so the two of them could go sailing around the Great Barrier Reef. One of the original partners wrote a nostalgic column about the *Chronicle*'s "true salad days, in more ways than one," describing Sloan as "our undisputed leader and, for all his all-too-human traits, the closest thing to the Spirit of '66 to tread sand on this rainy seacoast." A co-founder of Greenpeace hailed him as "a lead spirit of 1970, when the world changed for the better and forever." He was definitely an icon of the long-past love parade.

"He used to sit right where you're sitting, right about this time, every Tuesday, just like today," Sally said. She had folded up the paper and was looking out the window, chasing away tears. "The people would come in, and if a couple of them said, 'Great editorial today, Albert', he would bounce out of here like the king the world." She rubbed her eyes and sobbed faintly. "Oh, he liked to be stroked."

"Did you see any signs of it coming, Sally?"

She turned to me, her composure restored. "No. He was his usual self. Always had a quip; he had that dry British wit. He wasn't in last week, but it wasn't unusual for him to go a week or two between stops. I did see him last week, though. I don't know if he saw me. It would've been Friday."

"Oh, yeah?"

"Yeah, I was coming back from town, Stan was looking after the store. I took Joe Road from the highway, and I saw Albert in his little gold Volvo. But I don't think he saw me. He was turning up a driveway."

"On Joe Road?"

"Yes. Why? What is it?"

"Nothing. Around what time would you have seen him on Joe Road?"

"Let's see. It was just after two thirty when I relieved Stan. So that's ten minutes driving, then I put the groceries away and opened the mail. I would say about two fifteen, give or take five."

A pair of customers entered the store, and Sally sold gum and cigarettes to one, an ice cream sandwich and a Pepsi to the other. The smalltalk was just a buzz in my ear.

When they were gone, I asked, "Did you notice what driveway Albert pulled into?"

"There's a sign, on this side of it, facing toward the highway. It says fresh herbs and manure for sale, I think. But you know the property, the one with the big brown horse that keeps running away."

"All right. I know the horse. Came charging out of the bush one day while I was walking along Lower Road. Gave me a start. Looked at me then went galloping off in this direction."

"He's always doing that. The boys at the hall have had to tie him up more than once."

"But I didn't know where he came from."

"Yes, there's a woman that owns the place. I heard her name once—it's a funny sounding name, but I forget it. I don't recall her ever coming in. I see her driving a really old beater, a Dart, I think. I figured Albert was going there to buy something for Jan." Sally's face went numb as suspicion hooded her eyes. "But maybe Jan doesn't know about it, eh?"

"I'm sure either way, there's nothing to it. Maybe he was going to pick up an ad. He would drive to Dolphin Inlet to pick up a little business-card-size ad."

"Sure, it could be that."

"Still, I don't think I would mention it to anyone, because it could get back to Jan, considerably twisted."

"No, I won't," she gasped, her mouth a big O. "That's the last thing I wanna do. Start spreading malicious gossip about a dead man."

Sally turned back to the window while I sipped the last of my coffee. "Still nice and quiet out there," she said. "The faeries haven't come out yet."

The faeries were a new breed of "hippie", in the parlance of the old established hippies, who tended to despise the youngsters as welfare cases. They massed across the road at a health food restaurant, transforming the property into a medieval village square, complete with folk encounters on rough wooden benches and minstrels playing on the grass. The faeries apparently considered themselves actual faeries. Some of them had children whom they were raising to believe they were living faeries, too. They organized dances with live Celtic bands, festivals for Druid holidays like Beltane, and some of them indulged in designer drugs, presumably to expand their faerie consciousness. A few of them were also popping up as human chains at logging road demonstrations. Just like mom and dad.

It was past eight thirty, and the bad faeries might still have been sleeping off their ecstasy hangovers, but the customers were starting to roll in. I placed a toonie on the counter, smiled when I caught Sally's eye, got a chaste smile in return, and hoofed it back to the cabin.

IV: Miss Kewp

Twelve

I drove to Joe Road. It was shaping up to be a hot day. The road was surfaced in soft gravel, and the dust raised by passing vehicles had left an ugly grey film over the wild blackberries that grew in heavy clumps along the roadside.

The horse enclosure was visible from the road, and the sign was there as Sally had described it. I took the winding driveway slowly, as it was treacherous with potholes, and pulled in beside a fairly new-looking bungalow. The horse eyed me curiously from his pen, munching on hay, as I stepped out of the car.

Next to a very sloppy woodpile, a rusty red Dart baked in the heat. I knocked on the front door but got no answer, so I headed around to the back. I could hear music coming from somewhere. Behind the house, a row of sheds disgorged stacks of tarps, piles of green planters and mounds of topsoil.

I climbed a small staircase to the wooden deck and almost stepped on her thigh. It was a very nice thigh, beautiful in fact, and so was the rest of her, stretched out on the deck in dutiful submission to the morning sun.

Except for the cool shades, she was naked as a jay.

"Beg your pardon," I said, taking two steps back down the stairs. I was ready to turn away completely, though not quite committed.

She angled her head slowly on her stack of pillows, her mouth grim as she studied me from behind the shades. Then she lifted the glasses over shimmering blue eyes that held tender golden specks, and showed me a merry grin. "Hi," she said.

"Hi."

"You can come back up."

She shifted her hip so that I could get past, but other than that she didn't budge an inch. No, there was no girlish giggle. No quick streaking for the yellow cotton robe hanging a few steps away on the door hook. No absurd apologies. Instead she extended her hand in a rather graceful gesture and spoke in a peppy, slightly mannered voice. I placed the accent from somewhere around Toronto.

"I'm Pamela Grady. My friends call me Kewp."

I shook her warm dry hand.

"Pat Ross."

"In the flesh."

"Look who's talking."

She gave me that merry grin again, biting her tongue like some Chinese Buddhas I've seen. "Well," she said, "now you can say that you know, from direct observation, that I'm a natural blonde."

I sat down on a bench across from her, keeping my observation directly on her face. It was quite a face. Very fair, with a rosebud mouth and a strong little nose. High painted eyebrows and pronounced cheekbones gave it a wan Asian cast. Her corn-coloured hair was cut short and swept to the side. She looked to be in her early thirties, but her musical taste was somewhat older: Van Morrison's "Thanks for the Information" was playing in the background.

"What does Kewp stand for?"

"It's short for Kewpie Star Wars. It's a nickname I acquired in university. Something to do with being a doomed damsel in distress. A boyfriend had a dream, and in it I was killed by an Indian warrior. I was with a group of whites, and this war party was hunting us down, one by one I guess. I dismounted from my horse just as the warrior took aim, and then he came running after me. My hair was really long at the time, and my name in the dream was Kewpie Star Wars. But I still like it better than Pamela, and I loathe Pam."

"Kewp," I said. "Okay."

"And your name is Pat Ross. It's a great byline. I miss seeing it."

"You're a reader."

"Oh, I'm a fan. And I love writers in general. It's such a cerebral yet free-spirited occupation. Come on in, I'll show you something."

She put on the robe, giving me a lasting look at her high, smooth flanks, and led me inside to a well-appointed oak kitchen. It was nice and cool after the hot deck. I took a seat at the table while she poured us each a tumbler of apple juice. Then she told me to wait. I did so, eyeing a stunning Hindu tapestry on the wall.

She came back into the room holding a heavy embossed silver picture frame, eleven by fourteen. I recognized what was in it immediately—the two photos of Satchmo and the headline: "What a wonderful, wasted world". It was a full-page column I'd written at the *Star* back in November 2003. It was just after Winnipeg media mogul Izzy Asper had died and was written as a sort of tribute to the colourful, chain-smoking jazz buff.

"This is my favourite article," Kewp said. "I *had* to get it mounted. Let me read the opening."

And so she read tabby intro:

With everyone from the U.S. drug czar to Mothers Against Drunk Driving howling over the coming decriminalization of marijuana in Canada, we are faced yet again with a one-sided debate, as the illegal status of pot keeps its most credible defenders silent.

Indeed, when the PM begins joking about toking in his dotage, you know the lunatics have taken over the weed tent.

That's where a little history can help—in the form of a jazz story.

Something to let Grandma know that Reefer Madness *is really* Hello, Dolly.

That, yes, Satch was a viper, and his wonderful world was wasted, but it was wonderful all the same.

With touching shyness, she handed me the framed article. "Would you read the next part?"

I couldn't say no.

In the years after the Second World War, Louis Armstrong was bigger than popes or presidents. More than a jazz legend, he was the world's most beloved entertainer—a symbol to war-ravaged Europe of America's goodness, courage and indomitable cool.

No wonder that at the height of the Cold War, the U.S. State Department tried repeatedly to send Armstrong and his All-Stars to the Soviet Union to play; he was such an American turn-on.

He was also a daily marijuana smoker from about age twenty-seven until his death in July 1971, one month short of his seventieth birthday.

"We always looked at pot as a sort of medicine, a cheap drunk and with much better thoughts than one that's full of liquor," Armstrong told biographer Max Jones in his last years,

when he decided to "tell it like it wuz."

Armstrong, of course, couldn't tell it exactly like it wuz. He had to deny he was a present user, but he was unequivocal in his praise of "gage," as he called marijuana.

"We did call ourselves vipers, which could have been anybody from all walks of life that smoked and respected gage," Armstrong said. "One reason we appreciated pot, as y'all calls it now, (was) the warmth it always brought forth from the other person.

"If we all get as old as Methuselah, our memories will always be of lots of beauty and warmth from gage. Well, that was my life, and I don't feel ashamed at all. The respect for it will stay with me forever. I have every reason to say these words and am proud to say them. From experience."

I handed her back the frame, and Kewp accepted it like a tablet.

"Now, when I read it again, I'll hear you telling it to me in your own voice," she said. "Maybe sometime you can read me the part with the list. I love that list."

"You're a real sweetheart, Kewp, and yes, I'd love to read you the list sometime. But listen. I'm almost sorry to bring this up, but I should tell you why I'm here."

I saw a hint, or fear, of disappointment in her face as well. "I figured you'd get around to telling me."

"I'm tracking Albert Sloan's last movements—not for publication, I don't think, but as a favour to the family."

"Oh." She hid her lower lip, and her eyes fell.

"I'm not looking to expose any of Albert's secrets or anything like that. The fact is, Albert's family isn't convinced he took his own life."

When she heard that, Kewp raised her head, and her eyes were bold, burning almost. "Good," she said, making a little fist. "*Good.* I'm glad to hear they've got you involved, because I don't believe it either. Albert was here Friday, and there was nothing wrong with him. Nothing whatsoever. Unless he was told later in the day that he had a terminal illness, it doesn't make any sense to me, and I knew him well."

"You were friends, like?"

"Very good friends, I would say." She grabbed a handful of yellow hair and smoothed it back in place. "I have nothing to hide—you've already seen that. Albert and I weren't lovers. The truth is, he used to come here, and I would sell him a bit of whip."

"Whip?"

"Weed. I know some people who can get pretty nice stuff, reasonably priced. Albert, I guess he heard about me through a mutual friend and started coming here, oh, sometime early last year. His regular guy had moved into the city. He'd gone to him for years and years.

"So that's why he came. But he was also a friend; I'd say a dear friend. We had some wonderful talks, and he knew all kinds of stuff about subjects from horticulture to horses to Hinduism—and everything about the Coast. He was funny and bright. He had a great soul."

"How often did he buy off you?"

"Quite regular. Half an ounce, maybe every two, three weeks."

"That's a pretty heavy habit."

"I don't know. I think other people in his house smoked it too. It's about average for around here."

"But Jan, his wife, never came by with him, eh?"

"I've seen her around but never met her. He never introduced me. I don't think she wanted to know where the supply came from. Know what I mean?"

"Sure. Did Albert, by any chance, mention any stories he was working on? Anything he was looking into? Perhaps something that carried an element of risk?"

"Not that I recall."

"Did he say anything on Friday about some meetings he'd had in town earlier that day? Anything about Chief Charlie, Lars Lovedahl or Roy Barlow?"

"No, he never talked business with me."

"Did he ever mention anything to do with the poet Virgil Wood?"

Her eyes flickered. She gave it some thought. "He might have. I mean, I've heard about Virgil Wood, but I don't remember Albert mentioning him, at least not recently, except maybe briefly when he passed away."

"What about Settlers Road? The apple grove where he was found. Did he ever talk about that?"

She shook her head, not stopping while her eyes went deep inward. I was terrifying her.

"Sorry, Kewp. But you understand—"

"No, no, don't be sorry." She reached across the table and squeezed my hand, holding it in a firm grip. "I think what you're doing is right. I wish I could help, but Albert, when he was here, usually just talked about everyday stuff. And the world of ideas. Sometimes we'd have a hoot and just veg out on the deck. I can't think of anything he said, Friday or before, that might connect to what happened later. I swear it. I just can't."

I reversed the hand lock, giving hers the big squeeze. "You've been really decent with me, really open, and I appreciate it."

The cheerful radiance she exuded before we started talking about Sloan returned. "How could I hold anything back from Pat Ross?" she said in a husky, sardonic voice. She saw me looking at her stove clock. It was almost eleven. "You wouldn't be going into town, by any chance?"

"I'm going right through it."

"Would you mind dropping me? My car's an old beater, and it's on the fritz right now."

She ran upstairs and made it back in under five minutes, wearing jeans, a pink T-shirt, sneakers and a purple beret that worked dazzling wonders with the shade of red lipstick she wore. Foxy was the word.

I teased her about saying "on the fritz" half the way to Witka.

She also gave up her age: thirty-four.

Thirteen

I left Kewp smiling in her cool shades on Cowrie Street and drove to Dolphin Inlet. Turning off at the access road to the hatchery, I passed the Witka First Nation No Trespassing sign and spotted the dirty cream-coloured building on the shoreline below. I parked under the arches of a big cedar and hiked down a trail to the water.

This was where the inlet ended in a small muddy bay. I found a nice branch-covered area looking directly across at the hatchery, sat down on a log and waited.

It was just after twelve twenty when Lars Lovedahl's Ford Ranger pulled up. The big man wasn't alone. Two other men, dressed in dark business suits, one wearing a feathered grey fedora and carrying a briefcase, followed him through a blue side door into the building. Crazy Max was right on the money.

I stayed put for about five minutes. I was about to start heading around the rocky beach when I heard someone coming down the trail. A small denim-clad figure stepped out into the open, looked around and saw me. I didn't mind. It was old Marg, a reclusive salal picker who lived in a shack way up on the inlet. She was universally thought to be mad as a hatter. I'd given her rides from time to time, and we'd developed a friendly and occasionally valuable rapport. Marg was different, but she knew stuff.

She looked from me to the hatchery and back, then smiled with a knowing nod and sauntered over.

"Watchin' the parade?" she said.

"Trying."

She sat down on the log next to me. The stained peak of her red ball cap was turned down against the sun to protect her ruddy face, leaving only her large upthrust jaw exposed. "Sure I saw your car, figured as much."

"Lars Lovedahl arrived with two guys in suits. Know anything about them?"

"Them's vets. Danes, I hear. Come to check the fin rot."

"How bad is it?"

"Lookit there." She nodded to the water. "Least sixteen of 'em stocked in the inlet. Maybe five, ten thousand salmon per. Say six, be soft on 'em. Six times sixteen is what? You gone to school."

"Ninety-six."

"Ninety-six thousand rotten fish. Them Danes'll tell 'em how to sell 'em anyhow. They ain't gonna lose a whole crop, and 'sides it'd look bad."

"How do you know?"

"They tell me. They talk amongst each other when I'm around scroungin', cuz they don't care what I hear. And 'sides, some of 'em are hootin' mad about it. Say they were given guarantees."

"I can guess who gave them."

"You don't have to. That fat one did. His bunch."

I gave her a couple of cigarettes and thanked her for telling me what she'd heard.

"You just don't forget about my otters. Them sons killed off my babies, and I'd like to do the same back."

Marg, slowly puffing on a cigarette, drifted along the shoreline in the opposite direction from the hatchery. The blue door opened, and Lovedahl strode out with his two playmates. They all piled into the truck and drove off.

I changed my mind about trying to spy through the windows and hiked back up the trail. Three short-haired young Witka men were standing around my Grand Am. Each was dressed in a different coloured tracksuit. One was carrying a wooden crate; he was hefting it high, and it looked heavy. Another I recognized from around town. He called himself Superman, and he was bad news.

"Nice little Batmobile you got there, mister," he said as I stepped slowly toward them. "Too bad you don't even have one brain."

I had my eyes on Superman, so I didn't see it coming. The wooden crate slammed into my forehead, splashing me with foul briny water as I fell back. I had sense enough to roll toward the edge of the road as the kicks came, but that stopped when I hit the trunk of a maple. They kicked me in the back a few more times. The last one landed on my upper thigh, and I let out a shriek.

"Stay off reserve land, blue-eye!" Superman yelled. "I have three brains, and they tell me everything. Your one brain doesn't process, so do what I say and don't come back here again. You know I mean it."

I lay against the tree for a long time. The blows had stopped, and so had Superman's gibberish, so I figured they were gone. Down by the water, gulls were laughing loudly.

I tried getting up, but stabbing pain shot through my right leg, grounding me to my knees. I tasted blood and realized it was from a cut bleeding above my eyes. My head throbbed. At least the pain in my back wasn't so bad. Or maybe it was, and it was just that the other pains were so much worse.

I got up again and hobbled over to the car. I found a rag on the floor and used it to wipe the blood off my face. Then

I bound it tight against my forehead to stop the bleeding, tying it at the back. It held in place.

Getting my right leg into the car was murder, but once it was in, the pain gradually diminished and something close to normal feeling returned. I figured that was a good sign.

I drove the hell out of there.

At the edge of town, I turned on to the Coast Highway and was going to pull into a Mohawk station when I saw Kewp standing on the shoulder, bags of groceries at her feet. She was waiting for a minibus to take her back to Joe Road.

I pulled up in front of her and she came to the window. Her jaw dropped when she saw me.

"Holy! What happened to you?" She didn't wait for an answer. "Get out. Get out," she said.

I crawled out and she looked at me in horror, her nostrils flaring at the bad smell.

"What happened?"

"I was on reserve land."

She helped me around the back of the car, vigilantly waving away passing vehicles with her free arm, and opened the passenger door for me. She looked like she was going to start crying when she saw how I climbed in.

She drove. "Hospital?"

"No, home is fine. The pain is going. I'm sure nothing's broken. I just gotta get some ice on this leg and clean up. Sleep. I'll be okay."

She sniffed. "What's this awful smell? Did they throw you in the ocean."

"No, one of them hit me with a fish crate."

"Well, you're gonna have to shampoo your upholstery. And now I stink as bad as you." She looked at me sorrowfully. "I'm sorry."

I tried to laugh. "Why? You're sharing my ordeal and healing me with sheer personality."

I told her what happened.

"Idiot called me blue-eye. Do my eyes look blue?"

"No, I'd call them hazel. Green maybe. Not an ounce of blue." She turned on to Joe Road. "You're coming to my place for a little nursing."

I didn't argue.

The bright oak kitchen cheered me. Kewp went straight to the bathroom, started running a tub, making a racket opening and closing cabinets. "Take your clothes off," she called to me.

I did as I was told.

Kewp returned with a damp towel and removed the bloody headscarf. She gently wiped my forehead, frowning and pursing her lips. "The bleeding's stopped. It's not too deep. I'll disinfect and bandage it after you're out of the tub. Should be okay. You'll have two black eyes, though. Turn around."

She squatted behind me, gingerly touching the back of my thigh.

"Nasty," she said. "It's gonna be an ugly bruise, but ice will take care of the swelling. Let's get you in the water."

The lighting was muted in the steaming bathroom, produced by burning black and mauve candles arranged in groupings on all the flat surfaces. The water was thick with foam. Aromatherapy was in the air.

Kewp helped me into the tub. The warm water was an elixir. I leaned back against the foam pillow and felt no pain.

She took off her clothes, climbed into the tub facing me, and washed both of us with a sponge and a hand shower set at a gentle spray. When she was done she said, "Lean back," and I did.

She spun around in the water and slowly lowered herself against me.

I stroked her pink forehead, and she closed her eyes. I felt her floating breasts.

For about ten minutes we just lay there. Good Lord, it felt good.

Fourteen

I slept in Kewp's bed that afternoon. Once I thought I heard a man's gruff voice, angry, and Kewp laughing and saying, "Go to hell," but it went away as bad dreams do. I awoke to the smell of cooking, the faint sound of streaming folksy guitar and the pleasant clitter-clatter of a woman working in her kitchen.

The pain was gone, except when I turned and put pressure on my right leg, then I felt it.

Kewp came into the room and stood jauntily over me. Barefoot, in black silk pants buckled over a form-fitting pink lambswool sweater, she looked like a million bucks.

"Feeling better?"

"Much, thank you."

"Okay then. The big question is: Dylan or Van Morrison?"

"I thought it was Tolstoy or Dostoevsky."

"Another time, another race."

"I think your question is, too. But if you put it to me I'd have to say Van. The voice carries the day."

Kewp seemed to accept that. She pointed to an open closet. "Your clothes are all clean and hanging up. I shampooed your front seats and rolled down your windows. Should be dry by morning. I made a seafood lasagna that'll be ready whenever you are."

She kissed me on the forehead and left the room.

She was a good cook; the pasta and sauce were from scratch. There was a tasty artichoke salad, homemade garlic bread, cold white wine.

Later we had coffee on the deck, and Kewp smoked a joint. I declined.

"I thought I heard you arguing with someone today. A guy with a big voice."

"You heard right. That was Big Bill. He's an old friend, a last wave draft dodger. We *were* seeing each other for a while, but that was a long time ago. Big Bill's never let go. He still wants to own me. He saw your car and tried to make an issue out of it. I told him to get the hell out."

She insisted I walk the leg. We took a trail through the bush, crossed Lower Road and took another trail that led to a high bluff over the sea. It was a great spot; the only building we passed was an abandoned shack. The wind was blowing hard, so we sat between two big rocks in a patch of moss and dogwoods. Kewp smoked another joint. Again, I declined.

We sat there and watched the sun go down over the great leviathan of Vancouver Island.

"You know," I said. "It was originally named Quadra and Vancouver Island, giving top billing to the Spaniard who saw it first. Then the Brits conveniently shortened it. Clever, huh?"

"Typical," Kewp said. "When I took history at Ryerson, I realized that the British Empire was not much different from the Third Reich, except that they pulled it off and did it with panache."

"I'm sure all my Irish ancestors would agree with that."

"Mine, too."

"But my English forebears would probably balk."

"Mine, too."

Night comes down fast under those mountains. I led the way back.

"You're moving better," Kewp said.

Back at the house, I rolled up my car windows and felt the front seats; they were still damp. I went inside the house, where candles illuminated every room. Kewp insisted on again icing the leg. Then she gave me a glass of brandy to drink and sent me to bed.

"I couldn't sleep," I said.

"Then read me the list. There's a reading lamp next to the bed. Go up, climb in and get toasty, and I'll join you in a minute."

Five minutes later, she came into the room and handed me the framed article. Then she undressed—it was the third time today I would see her stitchless—and climbed in beside me. She blinked and smiled up at me like a little girl.

"Okay. I'm ready," she said.

I started reading from where I'd left off.

Armstrong's experience with marijuana warrants public exposure, because it counters so many clinical stereotypes.

Armstrong was well on his way to being a recognized musical giant before he took his first regular toke—his scrappy, soulful and downright demonic-paced Hot Five and Hot Seven "race records" of the 1920s had established him among musicians as the preeminent jazz soloist of his generation and a brilliant original singer.

After starting his forty-three-year association with marijuana in 1928, the mature Armstrong

• Entered his "classic" phase, teaming up with a young Earl Hines on piano to record the body of work that jazz critics consider Armstrong's—and therefore jazz's—finest. Among the jewels were "West End Blues", which some rate the best jazz record ever made, and a dreamy number called "Muggles", which just so happened to be slang for marijuana.

• Radically and permanently expanded the jazz songbook

to include pop standards, endearing himself to a largely white audience with songs like "When You're Smiling", "Ain't Misbehavin'", "Rocking Chair", "Body and Soul" and "All of Me".

• Transcended the record industry's segregated label system, opening the door for other black artists.

• Wowed New York and then Hollywood, appearing in dozens of films including Pennies From Heaven *(1936),* A Song is Born *(1948) and* High Society *(1956), for which Cole Porter wrote two Armstrong numbers. He also made a handful of three-minute music videos called "soundies" in 1942.*

• Worked with such diverse talents as Billie Holiday, Danny Kaye, Duke Ellington and Bing Crosby, who once said: "Rev. Satchelmouth is the beginning and the end of music in America."

• Reinvented the New Orleans sound with his All-Stars at landmark 1947 concerts, standing pat in the face of bop and other "fancy" musical trends.

• Travelled the world with the All-Stars, performing more than 300 nights a year and planting jazz and its offshoots in the U.K. and beyond, doing what he called "my day's work, pleasing the people and enjoying my horn."

• Became, in February 1949, the first jazz musician to appear on the cover of Time.

• Recorded some of his best albums, including classic duets with Ella Fitzgerald, in the '50s and enjoyed his first million-selling hit, "Mack the Knife", in 1955.

• Knocked the Beatles from their 14-week hold on No. 1 with "Hello, Dolly" in May 1964—more than four decades after his first recordings were cut with King Oliver's Creole Jazz Band.

Worshipped by musicians, adored by the public and loved by the people who knew him (including ex-wives), the mature Armstrong's career was dazzling, his life positively storybook.

And through it all, he smoked his gage.

I stopped there, and Kewp ran her fingers adoringly through my hair. "'He smoked his gage.' I love that. 'He smoked his gage.' And I love how he took out the Beatles when he was in his sixties, and they were at their peak of popularity. Finish it," she said.

I sighed but continued.

Despite his habit, he was always a meticulous professional, dependable, emotionally stable and universally cherished for his folksy wit and wisdom.

The only time the pot ever had overt negative consequences was in November 1930, when Armstrong was busted smoking a joint in the parking lot of the New Cotton Club in Los Angeles. He spent nine days in the city jail awaiting trial, and his record company sent an eastern gangster named Johnny Collins to L.A. to "fix" the problem.

"Whether he used sweet reason or hard cash, Collins did the job," wrote Jasen and Jones. 'Louis received a suspended sentence and went back to work and back to pot. He never smoked it in a public place again, but he would smoke it every day for the rest of his life."

Even in jail, Armstrong encountered some fellow vipers.

"We reminisced about the good ol' beautiful moments we used to have during those miniature golf days," he said. "We'd go walking around, hit the ball, take a drag, have lots of laughs and cut out."

You can say Armstrong did it to feel good—call it recreational if you like.

Or you can point to the unimaginable poverty of his childhood, the racism of his time, and say he used it as a crutch to take the edge off life's pain.

You can risk ridicule and say he did it because it helped connect him to the truth as a man and an artist.

You can definitely say it's too bad he smoked so much—he died of heart failure and, like the late Israel Asper, might have lived on for another decade if he hadn't smoked like a chimney.

But no one can say the mature Armstrong should have been denied his daily muggles—any more than you could have denied Asper his daily packs.

They came and went in clouds of smoke.

End of jazz story.

Fifteen

Kewp took the frame out of my hand and set it down on the floor on her side of the bed. Then she reached across me and switched off the reading lamp. "'End of jazz story,'" she said in the dark.

Her arm swam around me, and she pressed her lips against my shoulder. I just lay there on my back. After a while she asked, "What's the matter, Pat? You're stiff all over, except where you should be."

I gently removed her hand. "Sorry, Kewp. It's not you. It's a lingering illness called marriage."

"You're married?"

"Technically, I'm still married. But we've been separated for almost a year."

"A year? That's a long time to be carrying a torch, my friend. I was married too, once. It took me a while after the split to feel normal again, and have normal relations, but usually after six months, you're ready to move on. She must be a hell of a woman."

"Caroline was my wife for more than twenty years. We were still just kids when we met. Got married fast, started a family right away, struggled for years and then, just when our children were grown up, she tossed me out. I'd become an insufferable human being."

"You?"

"Yes, me. Oh yeah, I'd look good in print, coming on like Braveheart for every lost cause and hard luck case that had a little sex appeal. But believe me, all the good I had, I gave at the office."

"Did you cheat on her?"

"Not that, but everything else. I was verbally abusive. A bully. I neglected her. I made her feel small in different ways. I hurt her and gave her cause to suspect me, for sure. And part of the problem was definitely the weed. After the kids got to a certain age and weren't around as much, I started smoking to unwind at night. It got to be quite a regular thing. That's when the real lowdown nasty behavior kicked in. When I became useless. Of course, I didn't see it that way at the time. Too full of myself.

"Then I got out on my own, cleaned up and took a look at what I'd done to my life. What I had, and how I'd treated it. Like it was all for nothing. Suddenly I hated my job. Couldn't stand my voice, and that was the job. I went over to the house and begged Caroline to take me back. Cried like a baby, promising it would all be different—and I'm sure it would've been. But she'd taken enough and said no way, Charlie. Never again. And she's held to it ever since."

"Has she—moved on?"

"I don't think so, but I can't be certain. I don't talk to her very often—she took a management position, and she's really absorbed in it. I only see her briefly when I go over there to visit Clay, our youngest. He's the last one still at home. The other two, Jack and Fran, are in Alberta, working and going to school."

"You guys did start young. So you quit your job and moved to the Coast?"

"We had the cabin on Beach Road as a summer place. I used to come up here with my dad when I was a kid. The earliest memory I have of the Coast is the summer of 1967. 'Windy' by the Association was the big hit."

"That's old. So did you come here to work for Albert at the paper?"

"Not at all. I write freelance now, mostly for the U.S. market. Going to work for Albert meant taking a pretty big pay cut. No, I stumbled into the *Chronicle* gig a couple months after I got here. I started hearing things about what was going on in the bush and on the water. None of it was making it into print. So I approached him, and he hired me. I like guerrilla journalism, and I got to do some. And I liked the guy. He had a way with him."

"So do you. And I think you're way too hard on yourself. It takes two to tango, baby."

"Tell me something, Kewp. Do you think Albert was planning to leave Jan?"

She sat up and regarded me coldly in the semi-darkness. "What? You don't believe what I said about me and Albert?"

"No, you've got me wrong. I have no reason to doubt you. It's not that. Albert left some notes behind—that's how I found your house. It was like a to-do list for his last day."

"I was on the list?"

"He'd written 'Joe R.', and we thought it was a person. I figured it out because someone had seen him driving down Joe Road that day. But the last entry was also very obscure. It was 'Sayonara Jan.' That's why I asked you the question, in case he had mentioned anything."

"I see." She was back on my shoulder. "'Sayonara Jan' does make it sound like that. Or that he did plan to—"

"I know."

"But he sure didn't say anything to me about it." She lay quiet, thinking. "Could he have meant Sayonara Gardens?"

"What's that?"

"A garden centre, silly. A place of business. It's on the other side of the highway, on Taylor Road. About two miles up."

"Never heard of it."

"It's only been around for a couple years at most, but it's attracted a sort of cult following. It's run by a Japanese family, the Shimizus. Harry Shimizu's the boss. He knows anything and everything you could possibly want to know up here about plant care and growing a healthy garden. Oh, and his bonsais are works of art."

"And you think Albert knew about it?"

"I know he did. He told me about it. I had some shrubs out front that were dying a slow death, and Albert sent me to Harry. Harry fixed me up."

"Maybe that's it, Kewp. I'll go up there tomorrow and check it out."

"You better get your sleep. You might have a big day tomorrow. But try not to get beat up, okay?"

"I don't know about that. That bath was almost worth the beating."

We slept close and warm.

Kewp cooked me pancakes for breakfast. While we were eating, she asked, "About what you were saying last night, about weed. Are you saying that you don't believe any more what you wrote in the Satch the viper article?"

"I even had misgivings after I wrote it. An editor in the States was putting together an anthology of drug writings for a fairly major publishing house and asked if he could include it. He was quite gung-ho. I always said yes to those sorts of requests, but for some reason I didn't go for it. The book's out now and is getting great exposure. But I didn't want, even then, to put that article out there. And I was a regular user at the time."

Concern showed in her face.

"I still believe in having tolerance toward people who

smoke weed," I said, "and I don't support prohibition. I may have idealized Armstrong's habit, though. It's almost impossible, I think, to really know the truth about a person's life. But no matter how you slice it, I was advocating daily pot smoking, and for me that was the road to nowhere. When I was on it, I traded in my sense of purpose. Lost track of past, present—feelings. The everyday mind is a gift from God. Unfortunately it took me a lot of years and a lot of bags of grass to figure that out, and I still get the craving now and then."

"But you can say no."

"I can, and I do."

"Well, I still think 'What a wonderful wasted world' is right on."

"Well, I think you, Pamela Grady, aka Miss Kewpie Star Wars, are more than just right on. I think you're outta sight," and I reached over to give her a kiss.

She pulled my head across the table and gave me a longer, better one.

"Now when I taste maple syrup," she said, "I'll think of that kiss."

She waved merrily from the door as my car jounced up the cratered driveway.

The brown and black stallion was prancing restlessly around the pen, angling close to the fence in measured passes like a jet nearing takeoff.

I rounded the curves of the driveway and saw the tan Valiant with the green vinyl top blocking the exit. Valiants were the beaters most favoured by aged Coast hippies. A burly giant answering that description slammed the car door and approached me with a purposeful stride. This had to be Big Bill.

"Spent the night, did you?" he said in a menacing growl.

I said nothing.

He bent his face to the window. "Listen, bud. Kewp and I have had our differences, and we're going through a rough patch right now, but you better listen up. Kewp is my woman, and if you have any ideas otherwise, you're gonna have to go through me first. Do you diggy, bud?"

I said nothing. His big paw came through the open window and rested on the doorframe.

"You think you're Charlie Bronson? You don't even know Kewp. She brings in her jerks like you for a while, but she always ends up calling Big Bill to the rescue. Big Bill and his little bag of white. And I come over, and you know what? We snort and fuck for three days and three nights. That's my Kewp. You should see how she looks after the coke wears off. Not so appealing, bud."

"Move your car," I said, "and let me pass. And if you don't remove your hand now, I will kneecap you."

I touched the automatic lock and he jumped back at the whirring sound. He was flustered. Before he could say anything more, I rolled up the window. I'd heard enough from Big Bill.

Eyeballing me sheepishly, he climbed into his beater and spun hard in reverse, braking on the road in a swirl of angry dust. I drove past him and pointed the little Batmobile toward the highway.

It struck me that Big Bill was a dead ringer for the "biker-looking fella" that the old Scot had seen with Albert in the apple grove.

V: What's in a Tree?

Sixteen

Harry Shimizu was standing behind the counter explaining the care of perennials to an older woman, who was hanging on his every word.

He was a small, slender man in his fifties with white flecks in his spiky black flat top and a habit of blinking with his whole face as he spoke.

A red-haired Japanese woman I assumed to be his daughter was ringing up sales at the other end of the counter, quizzing the customers with easy efficiency to ensure they knew what to do with their purchases. She looked to be in her late twenties: petite, with a wild bottom and a long, small face that economically conveyed a wealth of hidden charms. Once, between transactions, she caught her breath and glanced my way, almost decking me with a brash crooked smile.

"Yes, sir, can I help you?" Harry said primly when my turn came.

I kept my voice down. "Hi. You're Harry Shimizu?"

He nodded.

"I'm working for Mrs. Sloan, the widow of *Coast Chronicle* publisher Albert Sloan, who died last week. We think it's possible he planned to come here Friday."

"He *did* come," Harry said, with unexpected force. "He came to check out the bonsai he'd ordered for his missus. Had it all paid for and everything. Here, I'll show you."

He led me to a connected greenhouse, where about three dozen miniature trees sat on low wooden benches close to the window. Placed on the floor were a few larger ones, including a couple of four-foot emperors. Kewp was right. Each one was a work of art.

"This is the one," Harry said, blinking fiercely.

It didn't register at first—it was too strange. I crouched down and studied it at eye level. It was unbelievable. It was the tree. It was a replica of the wishbone-shaped apple tree with the Atlas arms that Sloan had hanged himself from on Settlers Road, scaled down to about eighteen inches in height and breadth.

"He gave me the specs on it," Harry said. "After I heard how he died, I just couldn't bring myself to call the family. I was going to mail off a credit voucher, after a suitable time had passed."

"That was thoughtful of you, Harry. I could see how it might upset the family. For sure."

"Well, yes, especially considering."

"Well, yes. How did you make it such an exact replica?"

"Oh, it's not that exact. It's a different variety."

"To an untrained eye, it appears pretty close."

"Mr. Sloan brought in a picture; he'd taken it with a digital camera. I didn't have anything like it, so I picked up this crabapple in the city, in New Westminster actually. It conformed to the basic shape. I repotted it and trimmed it so that it would look pretty close. I worked from the picture Mr. Sloan brought me."

"You did a remarkable job. Did he tell you why he was so interested in that particular tree?"

"No, just that he wanted a bonsai that looked just like it."

"He didn't talk about Settlers Road or anything?"

Harry was thinking. Thinking and blinking. Blinking and thinking. "No. He just wanted to give it to his wife. A surprise."

"He gave her a surprise all right. Can I take it with me?"

"You're going to show it to her?"

"She would want it, and she can handle it. She's a strong woman."

Harry seemed torn about letting it go. "Well, you're working for the lady, so I guess it's okay." But he still hesitated.

"I should take it, Harry."

"Fine. I'll wrap it so it doesn't soil your car."

We went back to the counter. He handed me a brochure about caring for the bonsai and said he or his daughter would be happy to answer any questions if Mrs. Sloan had any. He placed the ceramic pot in a recessed cardboard tray that firmly secured it. While he gingerly wrapped the tree in green paper, I asked him when Sloan had ordered it.

"Last month," he said. He held up the invoice. "July 12."

"Fast work."

"Like I said, I was pretty lucky to find one that conformed roughly to the shape."

"How did he seem Friday?"

"He just came in to pay for it and said he would be back on the weekend to take it home. He acted like he always did, friendly but in a hurry. Here you go. Thanks for stopping by."

Handing me the package, Harry seemed eager to emulate his description of Sloan: friendly but in a hurry. He turned to greet a waiting customer, sliding a glance my way before surrendering to an explosion of blinks.

The daughter swung around her end of the counter and held the door open for me, soberly eyeing the wrapped bonsai. "Hi," she said quietly as I went past her. "Come again."

It was another balmy day. As I drove into Witka, I found myself singing an old camp song:

Ain't gonna rain no more, no more,
Ain't gonna rain no more.
How the heck can I wash my neck
If it ain't gonna rain no more?

A weathered red Dodge Ram pickup truck rode high on my tail then quickly pulled back, right turn signal going. The horn hooted twice. Max Riverton was at the wheel, and his right hand was pointing to the right as he did a lasso movement in violent rotation.

I got the message, Max.

The turnoff was thirty metres ahead. We both pulled into the Foster Creek Campground entrance and parked in the new landscaped section near the store.

Max hustled over to my window, a dark-eyed, tight-lipped, private man in his forties, about five-six with a bit around the beam. He was always clean-shaven and neatly conservatively dressed for the outdoors, his black curls scalp short. He was wearing a blue quilted waterproof vest over a cotton check shirt and saying "dirty *ba*stards" repeatedly after he saw my face. I got the story in where I could. When I finished, Max said, "They were carting off samples, I'll bet you money. That's what they hit you with. Samples from the infected stocks."

Max's deduction made my stomach turn. I shrugged.

Max insisted, "Those bastards were working for Lovedahl. People don't just get jumped like that on reserves. Have you ever been jumped on a reserve before?"

"Almost, once when I tried to stop this kid from pounding on a small fry. There was a woman there who took great offence to my intervention. The boys were cousins, she affirmed hysterically."

"Cousins? Oh, that explains."

"She gave me holy hell," I said. "Who was I to tell them to do anything? Who did I think I was? Who the hell did I think I was? The other reporters shuffled off. Then a group of the men started to make their way our way, so to speak."

"What did you do?"

"I got the hell out of there. But this was in the far interior. I still don't know what would've happened if the men had come over to investigate. They might've told that dame to quit sniffing unleaded. What I do know is the little prick was back pounding on the small fry when I was still in range to hear the wailing, so it became a real nightmare."

"I've never heard of it on the Coast. Whites go on that reserve every day, and nobody gets jumped like that. No, those were Lovedahl's shit-punks at work. What I don't get is this." Max pressed his knuckles deeper into his vest pockets. "Lars Lovedahl was fired, he doesn't hold any public office, but he's still here trimming up the shoreline leases and operating more openly than ever. You know what I mean?"

"Sure, Max."

"I don't see how this can happen. How can this happen?"

These cosmic questions make good quotes but lousy conversation. I telegraphed back: "I told Jake Jacobson about the outbreak rumours. He'll talk to someone pretty high up the chain in fisheries. Hopefully nothing bad will go to market."

"Eating goldfish, you take your risks. I don't call it salmon. How can you call it salmon?"

Max was getting mad. It's what he did, or what he'd say having his two-million-dollar view ruined did to him. It's why he spooked the media—Sloan called him "White Dwarf, the imploding materialist" or something—and probably why he'd lost his marriage and saw his daughter on arranged weekends. Being around mounting anger is intimidating, even if you know it's not aimed at you. You always think: I shouldn't have joked around.

I told Max my next stop was the Mounties, and I was going to make a report.

"Tell them I back you up. Use my name if you want."

"I will, Max," I said.

Seventeen

Staff-Sgt. Brennan was available; a bald corporal I'd never met buzzed me in and escorted me to his office. Brennan was behind the desk, wolfing salad out of a plastic container. He looked at my bandaged forehead and purply eyes and snickered.

"What have you been up to? Sloan's widow's called twice this morning. Wanted us to dredge the harbour for your corpse. Nice shiners, by the way."

"I got a crate in the face and had the boots put to me by a trio of Witka warriors."

"Why?"

"I was over by the hatchery, just looking around. They objected to that."

"You know you shouldn't be on reserve land unless you have business there."

"That's right. I had it coming."

"That's not what I said. Who were they?"

"I didn't see their papers, but I recognized one of them as a sniffhead who calls himself Superman."

"I think I know who they are. I'll let the other members know."

"Watch Superman. He's got three brains."

"What were you snooping around the hatchery for?"

"Max Riverton—"

"That crank."

"Even cranks get it right sometimes. Max told me Lars

Lovedahl was keeping company with a couple of Germans, and that they were up to something very hush-hush at the hatchery. A source tells me they're Danish vets trying to control a major vibriosis outbreak on the salmon farms."

"Better tell fisheries."

"Lot of good that will do. They're the ones that licensed them."

"Well, it's outside of our purview. You know that."

"I know. But it does prove one thing."

"And what's that?"

"Lovedahl was lying about Sloan's visit on Friday. Max had tipped Sloan off about the Europeans, and you can bet that's what Sloan was confronting him with."

"Maybe he was lying, maybe he wasn't. Everyone knows Lovedahl's a slippery character. Doesn't prove anything either way."

"How about a bonsai tree that looks identical to the one Sloan hanged himself from? Sloan ordered it last month, after Virgil Wood died. He was supposed to pick it up on the weekend. It's sitting out in my car if you wanna see it."

"All that proves is that he was nuts. Obsessed."

"And there's an old Scottish gentleman with a bad dye job who lives about four doors down from the apple grove, on the other side of the street. He says he saw Sloan and a guy resembling a biker on the property in late June."

"Sure, he hung out with druggies because he was a druggie. Mrs. Sloan told us about that, too. You're going around in circles in a white bowl, Ross. We got lab tests back from Heather Street; the widow was making such a big stink, we figured we'd cover our butts. Not only was that Sloan's rope, taken from a hook in his shed, but his prints are all over it, and no one else's. He tied the knot, he hitched the rope to the tree, and he put his head in the noose. And it wasn't a sudden job. He spent time on that knot."

Brennan got up and slapped his belly.

"But you should go over and see the Sloan woman. She's excited about something she found in an old back issue of the *Chronicle*. It's an article from way back—the 1940s, I believe. Some Witka wino hung himself way back when in the same spot."

"Really?"

He gave me a pitiful look. "Don't make it into a big thing. The woman's gone through enough. Looks like Sloan had marked the article, and that's how she came across it. He was looped, man. Something snapped, and he went cuckoo. This old suicide might have suggested a course of action. Maybe he identified with the wino; he'd been a drunk himself once by his own account. Try to get her off it. For her sake"—he looked at my messed-up face—"and yours."

Eighteen

The *Chronicle* office was practically deserted; it wouldn't start showing life until Thursday afternoon, but all hell wouldn't break loose until Monday, when they rushed to deadline. It was the institutionalized pace of an under-achieving weekly.

Jan was there though, sitting in Sloan's office with stacks of invoices, hard copy and old newspapers in front of her. She looked beaten down.

Relief, anger and alarm showed in her face when she saw me. She got up and practically nailed me to the wall. I told her about the beating and the Lovedahl angle and said I had something for her in the car. It all seemed to go past her.

"Where were you last night?" she demanded. "I kept calling and even went over to your place to see if you were okay."

"Sorry, Jan. I never thought of calling you, but I guess I should have. I wound up spending the night at a friend's, who nursed my wounds."

I didn't like the way she weighed my statement with her big dark eyes. There was an unmistakable air of proprietorship in the room, and I wanted to run.

"I heard you found something interesting about the apple grove," I said meekly.

Her intense stare finally wore off, but she remained aloof as she led me back to the morgue.

The *Chronicle* went back to the 1890s, but a fire had destroyed the saved copies prior to the Second World War. It was a bit of a tragedy, because old newspapers are a hoot to read, telling us more about their times and places than the people who made them could ever imagine. And in small towns especially, the newspaper was the primary, if not exclusive, historical record. In the case of the *Chronicle,* carefully bound copies for each calendar year started at 1945.

Jan removed the 1949 binder from the top of the first pile and explained she had found it that way, slightly askew on the neat stack, when she visited the morgue yesterday afternoon. At first she thought it had simply been misplaced—it should have been fifth down the pile—then she noticed a B.C. Ferries ticket stub sticking out.

"Albert often used those stubs to mark pages in books and reports. I scanned the page and saw this article."

I looked at the ferry stub. The ticket date was July 3, 2004.

The edition was dated April 11, 1949, and the article was little more than a badly written blurb:

WITKA MAN SUICIDES

Fueled by cheap whisky, a local Indian resorted to that most desperate of acts when he took his life last Thursday.

The body of Ezra Paul, 46, was discovered Friday morning on Settlers Road by civic employees arriving to work at the Witka Municipal Hall No. 1.

Clerk T. P. Houle was the first to see Paul hanging from a rope tied to an apple tree across the street from the old Hall. Houle alerted arriving firemen who cut the man's body down and covered it with a blanket.

The wretched native had been on a drinking binge in town the night before and made his way on foot to the edge of the former Barlow Orchards, where he did the deed.

An empty liquor bottle was found near the base of the tree.

An axe lay nearby.

Police chief Grant reported that Paul had stolen the axe from a farmhouse in the vicinity and made a half-hearted attempt to chop down the tree before abandoning that notion in favour of suicide. The rope was later found missing from the back of the fire hall.

Witka natives say Paul returned to the reserve that very day after an absence of many years, only to learn that both his brothers had been killed during the war. His parents had also died since he left the peninsula, and the grieving man found his only solace in a bottle and finally self-inflicted death.

His body was taken into the mountains below Dolphin Inlet for traditional Indian burial.

"So what do you make of that?" Jan asked me.

"I've never heard of a Paul family around here. Did you talk to Jerome Charlie about it?"

"No, I just told Brennan, and then I got kind of caught up in other things, like being worried sick that something bad had happened to you."

I squeezed Jan's arm above the elbow and told her, again, that I was sorry about putting a scare into her. I said I would talk to Jerome. Then I told her I was going to get something out of the car and bring it into her office.

She was standing beside Albert's desk when I returned. I put the package down in front of her, and she tore off the wrapping.

"I figured out what 'Sayonara Jan' meant. It didn't mean goodbye. It meant he was going to go to Sayonara Gardens and pay for a gift he wanted to give you. That's the gift."

"It's the tree," she said.

"Yes."

Tears filled her startled eyes.

"I know it's hard to accept this, Jan, but Albert might have been unbalanced. He obviously loved you right to the end, but I'm not sure he knew what he was doing."

Her face was a ghastly mask of pain. Words came out like slivers. "You're giving up?"

"Not yet," I said. "But we better get real here. This might not turn out the way you want."

She nodded. She knew.

I left her with Sloan's last gift.

VI: Ezra Paul

Nineteen

I stopped first at Venture-West, but the young woman at the desk in the front office said Lars Lovedahl was gone for the rest of the day.

"Any message?"

"Just tell him it was some beat-up white guy from the Danish embassy."

I drove onto the reserve. Jerome Charlie's wife opened the door. I'd met her once but couldn't recall her name. "Hi," I said. "Just here to see if I could talk to Jerome for a minute."

Mrs. Charlie was a tiny, nimble woman with a sly but likable face. She was dressed in a denim ensemble and wore a fair amount of makeup accented with loads of semi-precious jewellery—I spotted rose quartz and moonstone necklaces, a yellow jade pendant, clumps of green jade earrings, and a fat amethyst bracelet slung low on her slight brown wrist. The overall effect was rather pleasing. She regarded me, chewing mint gum meditatively. She had to be close to sixty.

"You'll find him down at the carving shed, behind the band office. That's where he spends most of his free time these days. He's not much fun to talk to, anyway."

"Been a tough year for Jerome."

"It is what you make it." She cornered the gum in her gaunt cheek. "He needed the break; I know I did. Jerome just don't want to admit it. That's why he's as miserable as all hell. It's what you do with what's given to you."

I nodded. Just then I remembered her name. "Well, I'll try the shed. Thanks, Kate."

"You're welcome, Pat," she said and closed the door.

Jerome was working with two younger men on the last unfinished pole. A compact dude with bandito whiskers and a barrel chest under his black T-shirt was hollowing out cheekbones with an adze, while a twin-spirited-looking guy in a Jackson Pollock smock was painting bright reds on unattached thunderbird wings lying on each side of the pole. It looked like they were making good time.

Jerome was straddling the pole about midway up, using what looked like a hunting knife to round off the bulging eyes of a shark.

He looked at me and said, "Now what do you want?"

"Can we talk in private?"

He led me through the back of the band office building to a small lunchroom with vending machines, a fridge, a microwave and a couple of untreated cedar tables.

I sat down at one of them, but Jerome stood over me. The knife was in a sheath looped on his belt.

"I just want to know what you can tell me about Ezra Paul."

He looked up in disgust. "Funny how you guys care about a dead Indian all of a sudden. Your boss asked me the same question when he came barging into my house last week. I'll tell you what I told him—no one remembers Ezra Paul. They sent a lot of the young people away in those days, first because of the smallpox and then because there was nothing here for them. They shipped them off to Squamish, the Mission reserve in North Van, even into the interior. They grew up not knowing who they were, only that they were worthless. The white man told them so."

"Come on, chief. Spare me the diatribe. I just want to know about this one guy who just so happened to take his life in the same place, in the same way that Albert Sloan did more than fifty years later."

"*Ezra Paul,*" he yelled, "Ezra Paul came back, and I guess he didn't fit in, didn't know anyone here. He got drunk and took his life. It's a sad story of my people, and really it's none of your business. It was none of Sloan's either, and I told him that."

"Well, he sure made it his business in a funny sort of way. Why didn't you mention it to anyone afterwards, when we were all wondering why Sloan came to see you?"

"It's none of your business."

I shook my head. "I used to go to bat for you. What happened to you, chief?"

"Quit calling me chief. I'm not chief any more, and when a white man calls a First Nation man chief, and he isn't a chief, he's using the title as a term of derision. It's disrespectful and racist."

"What's going on at the hatchery, Jerome?"

"What are you talking about?"

"The salmon farm people have big trouble."

"Don't ask me about that. Like I say, I'm not chief any more. You don't seem to understand. The hatchery supplies the farms. We've got signed contracts; it's business."

He opened the lunchroom door for me to follow him out, quickly scanning my face. "I see you've already run into the business end of something. You're sticking your hand into everybody's pies. Better be careful. You might come up a finger or two short."

Twenty

Both hands on the steering wheel, all fingers reasonably intact, I drove north along Dolphin Inlet.

Past the hatchery turnoff, past the last of the subdivisions, past the pavement and on to the rocky gravel—all the way to the end, to Hidden Cove.

Hidden Cove was the original Witka village. Back in the pre-contact days, the Witka had moved their camp to the open strait only for a few weeks when the sockeye were running. Then they moved back to their main village, which afforded them protection not only from the heavy weather but also from the northern tribes who raided the south for slaves and women.

A core of about two-dozen Witka families still lived at Hidden Cove, and I knew one of the matriarchs, Esther Henry, from my days at the *Star*. Esther had written to me a few years back with a hard luck story about her grandson. Norman was a commercial fisherman who had gone to Vancouver to find his two-year-old son. He found the boy but couldn't get custody, even though the mother had become a crack-addicted prostitute. The young man blew his savings on legal fees, hit a brick wall in the system and eventually wound up on the skids himself. Esther had lost touch with him.

I located Norman Henry, helped get him into an aboriginal-run detox program, then, once he was cleaned up, drew public attention to his cause and the plight of his toddler, who was living in one of the worst fleabag hotels on East Hastings Street. Within a week, the boy had been turned over to his dad, and the two of them were back in Hidden Cove, eating at Esther's table. Esther later wrote me a beautiful thank-you letter, and since moving to the Coast, I had driven up there a couple times and visited the family, accepting gifts of free fish, because I can't say no to free fish.

A woman in her twenties answered the door, giving me the concentrated deadpan reserved for strangers in these parts. She smiled quickly when I told her who I was; she'd heard about me. Her name was Louise, and she was Norman's girlfriend. I told her Norman was doing even better than I thought. I wasn't kidding either. Louise had some size, but she wore it well. Her apparent shyness about showing her nice teeth made her lovely face even prettier. Norman, she said, was out on the boat, and Esther had taken the little boy to check on the crab traps. The two of them should be back any minute.

I should have accepted her offer to wait inside, but I wanted to look at some new houses that were going up, and I always enjoyed walking along the plank sidewalk past the older homes on the water; they looked kind of rundown but also somehow extremely vibrant. As well, I wanted to have a smoke.

I was leaning on a white wooden fence between houses, enjoying my cigarette, when I saw them coming down the boardwalk. Three figures heading my way with "unbending intent"—like models for a Carlos Castaneda pocketbook cover. It was Superman and the Justice League, and they had spotted One Brain back in their domain, without a paddle.

I could have run, but my leg was still giving me quite a bit of trouble from yesterday's wind-up kick, so I wouldn't have made it far. Times like these are when you envy Americans for carrying guns.

Superman was shaking his head as they stopped a couple of feet in front of me. He was about to say something inordinately clever when a woman's sharp voice sounded out. "Get away from him, you sons of bees!"

It was Esther Henry, and she was hurrying along the boardwalk towards us. The three goons all turned their backs on me, and it was tempting to tear a loose plank off the fence and start whaling on them. But I took another drag on the cigarette instead and let Esther handle matters.

"You troublemakers have been told to keep away from this village. You're always looking for more, aren't you?" She looked at my face. "Did *they* do that to you?" I sucked in my mouth and nodded gravely.

Her expression was gold. "You little bastards," she told them. "Pat Ross has done more for our people than you bums will ever do in your lifetimes, if you live to be a hundred. Get the hell out of this village, and don't come back!"

Without a word, the goon squad took a hike.

"Pretty good," I said, "for a gal pushing seventy."

Actually, I'd shaved off a decade. Esther was pushing eighty, but her tiny frame, defiant grey head and smart mouth seemed to ward off the push of time.

"Why did those jokers beat you up like that?"

"I was spying on the hatchery."

"That place doesn't need spying. It needs dynamite."

My kind of woman.

Twenty-One

Inside the house, Esther brought her great-grandson into the front room to see me. Elijah was seven years old now and remembered me from past visits.

We said hi, then I was greatly shocked to discover a Matchbox car in my pocket, still in its package. Amazingly, it was a black Pontiac Grand Am.

"That's *your* car," Elijah said.

"Yes, but without the scratches."

He held it close to make sure about the scratches, then smiled like a fiend when he saw there were none. He ran into the kitchen to show Louise the toy.

Elijah came back and handed me and Esther each a can of cold Pepsi, then ran upstairs, going *vroom, vroom* on the banister. Gotta love kids.

We sat down and cracked the drinks open. After exchanging civilities, I told Esther what I was up to and got around to the Ezra Paul question.

"Who was he?"

"Who was he is right," she said. "There weren't many Pauls here. They were mostly a Capilano reserve family. I knew Betty Paul when I lived in Vancouver back in the forties and fifties. She was fat and not very bright, but a nice girl.

"The Pauls from around here died out way back. There were two boys, Enoch and Zeke. Their father died when they were kids. They both went overseas during the war, the Second War. Their mother died while they were fighting.

Neither one of the boys made it back."

Louise brought out a plate piled high with steaming crabmeat, two long skinny forks and a bowl of melted butter for dipping. Esther sat back on the couch for a while and just smiled, watching me go at it. Then she pushed forward and joined in. After a couple of mouthfuls, she called out to the kitchen, "Bring some of those pickles in, would you, honey?"

"Then who was Ezra?" I said.

She laughed. "There was no Ezra."

"Come again?"

"I was in the city at that time and was just a young girl trying to make my way, so I don't know what was going on back here. That's when they put the reserve next to the town, made it the big reserve. When I was a little girl, we never went to town for much, but the beach there has always been nice. We'd go for that. We'd go to town to have a swim." We laughed at her good one.

"Then my husband brought me back in 1958, and one day I heard about Ezra Paul dying out on Settlers Road. They said he was an older brother of the two boys, Enoch and Zeke. I said I knew the Pauls, and there was no older brother named Ezra. And somebody said, well, there must have been because he died. And I said, well, you've got to be alive before you can be dead, and he was never even alive. But they told me to shut up and forget about Ezra Paul."

"Would Jerome Charlie know all that?"

"He would know more than I do, although he was just a kid back then, but he lived there. His grandfather, Benjamin Charlie, was the first chief down at the new reserve, so the Charlies would know better than anybody about Ezra Paul." She wiped her mouth with a paper towel. "I don't know if I would ask them about it, though, because they might get mad. They were into different things at that time, and a heck of a lot of land was involved. When you got land involved, you got different kinds of trouble."

"Any idea who the dead man might have been, Esther?"

She laughed hard. "They told me it was Ezra Paul!"

Esther, Elijah and Louise all came out to the car to see me off.

Elijah told me that if he ever got lost in the woods, ravens would take care of feeding him. "I read him that story from the Third Book of Kings," Esther said. "About his namesake. Now whenever he sees ravens, he waves at them."

I shook the little boy's hand and kissed both ladies on the cheek. They all waved as I drove down the rutted gravel road.

VII: Telltale Flowers

Twenty-Two

Virgil Wood knew; that had to be it. Virgil knew who the dead man actually was.

It was late afternoon when I got back to Beach Road, and I let the car take me. It kept going past my driveway, past Seaview Market, on to Lower Road, and ended up parking me next to a brown house with a For Sale sign in front of it. It was the old poet's place.

I got out and walked around the property. Like Sloan's, the house was an old summer cottage with an addition. The old section was nice, though, with a glassed-in verandah facing the sea and a roomy, turreted second floor. Monkey-puzzle trees and stately rose bushes adorned the front yard; the back was simply spectacular.

An arbutus plank bridge, its handrails made of varnished driftwood, arched over herb and rock gardens, and a clear, active brook that fed into a network of lily ponds. The fantasia ended with a great lawn that swept into a gentle rise, where cherry trees planted at regular intervals seemed to guard the property from afar, like ancient warriors in their last stand against ocean and heaven.

I sat on a bench between two trees and marvelled at the man's vision and incredible good luck. Starting in a tin shack on the beach, he'd found paradise a stone's throw away and managed to hold on to it for what seemed like an eternity.

On cue, a neighbour started his lawn mower. I ambled over to the side of the property and took a peek over the hedge. I saw him from behind: big guy, shirtless, shaving his side of the sloped fairway in a yellow and green riding mower. Something about him was familiar. He veered his machine to the right, and I caught his profile. Tattooed arms, sandblasted beard and head, a face all too ready for trouble. It was Big Bill.

Staying close to the hedge to keep out of his view, I returned to my car. I got the digital camera from the glove box and went back the way I'd come. A sparse patch in the hedge gave me decent sight lines. I waited for him to swing by and got off a pretty good shot on the second pass.

I drove to Settlers Road and knocked on the old Scottish gentleman's door. He was wearing pants this time, but the mutt was still yapping. It broke through some kind of barrier and came charging for my feet, a frenzied Shih Tzu that flipped over joyfully after making contact, raising its little black face to me and barking out amazing stories. I made nice with the mutt— "Little lion," I said, "little *li*on"—and it calmed down, awaiting further adventure. That got me in the door.

Worry showed in the man's pale, lined face. "I went to the RCMP, like you advised. But they told me in no uncertain terms that I shouldn't discuss it further with anyone." He glanced at the dog, which listened like a third party, then added with clenched teeth, "Not even you, sir."

I nodded, agreeing with him wholeheartedly. "That's standard policy with all witnesses and informants. However, this case is closed, and I'm not here to ask you questions anyway. I just want to show you something."

I held up the camera with the viewfinder turned toward him. He peered into it.

"Hey, that looks like the biker fella."

"Yeah? Here, take another look."

I showed him a sequence of lesser images, then stopped again at the money shot.

He stared some more, sighed, then swivelled his head to play with the light source.

He sighed again and nodded. "It looks to be him."

"Good," I said, tucking away the camera.

A wild gleam darted from his eye. "Big bruiser, huh?"

"I'll say. Leave it with me for now. If they do decide to reopen the case, you might have to give another statement, maybe identify this guy if they care who he is. They might not. But for now, you're not even supposed to be discussing this, remember?"

I was almost at the street when he shouted, "And I didn't. I didn't discuss a damn thing."

I turned around and called back, "That's right."

The dog yapped excitedly from inside as if it knew they'd been had.

Twenty-Three

I didn't want to go home to cook, so I grabbed a mushroom burger, strawberry pie and coffee at the White Spot drive-in on the highway. It was just after seven when I pulled up at Kewp's house.

She opened the kitchen door and gave me one of those provocative lip-biting smiles. She was wearing a sleeveless orange summer dress, and her fine shoulders glowed with tan. "Glad you made it," she said. "Have you had supper?"

"Yes, thanks. Need to talk."

"That sounds serious."

"I think it is."

We sat at the kitchen table.

I said, "You haven't been straight with me about Big Bill." Kewp's eyes went up, and she was about to speak. "And I don't mean you and him," I cut in. "I mean about him and Albert."

"Ah," she said. She crossed her legs and remained silent.

"We have a situation here, Kewp, and I'm worried about it. I probably should be sitting with the cops right now instead of here. But I do feel I owe you something for yesterday, so I'm giving you a chance to level with me first."

She looked at the sink counter and coughed. When she spoke, her tone was carrying ice. "What is it you think you know?"

"Two things. Three, actually. First, that Big Bill was Virgil Wood's neighbour. Something you never bothered to mention when we talked yesterday about Wood. The second thing is the real worrying one. That Big Bill went to the apple grove with Albert back in late June. He's been identified by a witness."

"*To the cops?*"

There was real alarm in her voice, and at that moment I knew I was on dangerous ground. I half expected Big Bill to come bounding out of the shadows and finish me. Then there would be nothing to connect him to Settlers Road.

"No, not yet," I said.

"What's the third thing?"

"Let's just talk about the first two first."

Kewp rubbed her mouth, thinking about it.

"Trying to come up with a story, Kewp?"

"No!" she snapped. "I'm *trying* to figure out if I should expose my life to you and maybe risk going to jail. How's that?"

"I don't know, because I don't know what you're talking about."

"Come with me," she said, sneering, as if I'd asked for it.

I followed her out of the kitchen. She strode into the laundry alcove next to the bathroom and pulled the cord on an overhead bulb to reveal a big clothes closet against one wall. She swept the coats and jackets aside, pushed the back of the closet, and walked through the opening. I went in after her.

The brightness from the grow lights hurt my eyes, and the smell almost knocked me over. It was like stepping into an indoor forest of sticky, ornately budding marijuana plants. Wedged between the pots, several oscillating floor fans made a terrific hum.

"This is what I do," Kewp said. "I have three other rooms like this in the house. Six lights in each room. One reason I use candles all the time is to keep my hydro bill as low as possible, because that's a way they can track you. It doesn't make much of a difference, I suppose, more psychological than anything.

I'm lucky, though, because this house is zoned as a duplex, and I pay my hydro on two separate bills."

I was looking at the plants.

"This looks like Grade-A stuff," I said.

"It is. I have a pretty small operation, but I grow the best B.C. bud there is." She turned to me, and the old friendliness was back. "Too bad you don't smoke any more, Pat, because this stuff would really get you high."

"I'll bet."

"I try for three good harvests a year. This crop is past due already. I was planning to cut it down on the weekend, but when I heard the news about Albert, I thought it might be a good idea to postpone. Partly out of respect, but also because I knew someone might be coming around to ask questions, and for a few days this whole house will just reek of pot. I didn't think it would be you showing up, I'll tell you that."

We went back to the kitchen. Kewp made tea.

"Big Bill got me started after I moved here—he's been growing prime bud longer than almost anyone on the Coast. He brought me the choice cuttings. You can't grow stuff like that from seeds; you have to start with cuttings. He taught me the basics of plant husbandry and set me up with a buyer in the city."

"He went all out for you."

"We were seeing each other in those days, but this is business for Big Bill. He's set up grows like this all over the Coast, and he gets a cut from each one. He's our original benefactor, and he always gets his cut."

"But what does that have to do with Albert?"

"Nothing. It's just that Big Bill can't take any heat. Bill and Albert were friends. They met over here, and they used to see each other sometimes over at Virgil's place. They actually had a lot in common."

"Really?"

"Both intelligent, well-travelled men who did things their way."

"Sorry, but my exposure to Big Bill, brief though it was, didn't bear that out, Kewp. He struck me as an ape. And he has no class whatsoever in regards to you, my dear."

"Oh, I know. On the subject of me, Big Bill is a big loser. But you don't get where he is without having a lot on the ball."

"So you're saying that whatever he knows about Albert's death, he can't share it because it would bring the law to his doorstep."

"He doesn't *know* anything about Albert's death," she said shrilly. "I've talked to him about it. He's actually afraid for his own life, because they were both hanging around Virgil and listening to his stories."

"What kind of stories?"

"I don't know. Neither one of them told me."

I must have looked skeptical.

"I'm telling you the truth. I think it started as Albert's thing; Big Bill just got interested in it this summer. They sort of teamed up for a while, but the last few weeks, Big Bill says he didn't see Albert or talk to him. But he won't tell me what he knows, absolutely refuses. I mean, here's a guy with biker connections, Hells Angels connections, he's a pretty tough motherfucker, and he practically starts trembling if you ask him anything about it."

"He could tell me off the record."

"You don't know Big Bill. That's what he was yelling about right here in this room yesterday when you were upstairs sleeping. I told him you were trying to find out the truth about Albert's death, and he said to get you the hell out of here. He said you're bad karma, and he felt death when he came to the house and saw your car here."

"Too much drugs."

"Maybe. What was that third thing you mentioned?"

"I guess I shouldn't tell you."

"Tell me."

"You might be doomed if you hear it."

"*Tell me.*"

I told her about the reported suicide of Ezra Paul, and how I had reliable information that strongly suggested another man had died in the apple grove back in 1949.

Kewp took it all in with a look of terror and wonder. "That must be what Virgil talked to them about," she said. "That *is* creepy. Now you have to spend the night here."

"I can't, Kewp. I have to go home. In fact, I hate to spook you and run, but I really ought to get going."

I gave her a small perfunctory hug before I left and told her that her secret was safe with me. I didn't mention that there was a chance the Mounties could come knocking on my door asking about the lawnmower man. No use making her crazy with worry. I was, after all, bad karma on wheels.

Twenty-Four

There were three phone messages when I got home. Two were hang-up calls, but both times the party waited awhile, with aboriginal drums beating in the background. The third was Ian J. Cameron, the *Chronicle*'s bitter ex-ace ad seller, wanting me to call back pronto. He sounded angry.

I called him. His wife answered and went to get him without saying hello back. Tish didn't like newspaper people. One reason, I guess, why I'd never been inside his house, even though I'd stopped there several times to visit.

"Didn't think you were going to return my call," Ian said.

"Just got home. What's up?"

"Well, I was in town, and I heard tell that you were back on the *Chronicle* payroll, working on behalf of grieving widowhood."

"So?"

"So, you didn't tell me that when you were by here the other day."

"I talked to a lot of people that day, Ian, and I guess I lost track. But so what?"

"So what? So what? You think I would've even talked to you if I knew you were working for *her*?" I heard Tish's voice in the background uttering a cautionary "*I*an."

"I wasn't collecting evidence against you, Ian."

"'I wasn't collecting evidence against you, Ian,'" he mimicked. "Maybe not, but you *were* collecting evidence, you just admitted it. She's got you playing Sam Spade, as if that shit's life was worth taking. But hey, if we need someone to frame it on, why not ol' Ian? He hated the goof—everyone knows that—and he just lives right on down the road." He paused to emit a disgusted breath. "I guess you went back to her and told her everything I said."

"As a matter of fact, I didn't. You didn't say much anyway."

"Whatever. But hey, I picked up something else in town, and you're welcome to try this on. I heard the goof was spending a lot of time with a bimbo on Joe Road. Sounds like the old bloke was working some New Age pussy on the side. Crystals and chips, my deah? Hope the bimbo had her shots. But what I was really thinking: if Mrs. Goof knew about that, I'd call that motive. Big time. Make *that* broad jealous, and we're talking dangerous furry animal, son. Something to maybe take back to your client as a working hypothesis."

"Is that all, Ian?"

"'Is that all, Ian?' No, one more thing. Who saw him last, and now who thinks he was killed? Think about that. Only the killer would know, so only the killer would want to cover his—or *her*—ass just in case the Mountie forensic geniuses actually turn up something. By hiring you and hassling the cops to look into it, she's already made herself look above suspicion. Oh, and if Joe investigative reporter does find out anything, she'll be the first to know, won't she, Joe?

"So, to sum up. It boils down to this. Either you're wasting your time. Like an idiot. Or you've climbed into bed with a rattlesnake. I just hope you're an idiot. Sweet dreams."

He hung up. I wondered what his wife would say to him after hearing him speak that way. Or maybe she didn't mind, or hated the Sloans as much as Ian did. I never could figure out people from Ontario.

I had a smoke on the porch. It was night now, and black clouds were piling up behind the trees, taking out the stars.

You could smell the rain coming on the wind. I went back inside and called Jan's number. She was home.

"Just checking in," I said. "Any developments on your end?"

"Nothing worth mentioning. What about you? Did Jerome Charlie say anything?"

"No, but I got some stuff from other sources. Why don't we have lunch tomorrow and go over it?"

"Fine. Tomorrow's going to be insane, but I'll clear the deck from twelve to one."

"Thanks. By the way, Jan, who've you told that I was looking into Albert's death?"

"No one. Practically no one. I mean, I told Sgt. Brennan. I didn't tell Albert's family. No one at the paper. Oh, that's not true. I told Rita."

"Rita?"

"Yes. She was asking why you stopped by today, and I told her what you were doing. She *swore* she wouldn't tell anyone else. Is there a problem?"

"I'm not saying there's a problem, but the best policy—in fact, the only policy—is to tell no one anything. Word always travels. So say nothing. That goes for anything I tell you, okay?"

"Okay. I'm sorry."

"Nothing to be sorry about. I've had to share information too, but only when I had to. We'll see you tomorrow."

"See you then."

Rita. Rita.

Twenty-Five

I slept badly. Shouldn't have had the White Spot burger. Stick to fish, stupid.

I had an awful dream. I was in the backyard. It was night, and rain was blowing hard. I was flying around and stopped in front of the big pear tree. A man was bound to it, arms and legs outstretched, like he'd been tied there for days, weeks, exposed to the elements. Rags clung to his skeletal frame, caked in mud. He was an Indian, a whale hunter I figured, with huge matted hair billowing back, his face clenched in agony. We looked at each other, and I knew there was no escape. He knew it, too.

I woke up and heard the rain pounding on the roof and the walls of the cabin. The alarm clock said 2:47.

My feet got drenched when I went to close the window, but I stood there for a minute anyway and peered into the outer darkness.

The pear tree was rattling, performing wild bows to the wind.

I went into the bathroom, turned on the light and towelled my feet dry. I looked at my face in the mirror and was almost surprised to see that it wasn't caked in mud.

I turned off the light and climbed back into bed. Just as I closed my eyes, the phone rang in the kitchen.

I answered it on the third ring. "Hello."

No one spoke. Native drumming and spirit song sounded in the background.

"Hello."

The party hung up.

I kept the lights off, but I didn't go back to bed.

Instead I made coffee and sat by the kitchen window drinking it, smoking cigarettes and keeping watch on the darkness.

After I settled down, I wrote a little column in my mind.

For some reason, the bound man in the dream reminded me of Macuina, the Nootka high chief responsible for the worst massacre, at least to my knowledge, in the recorded history of the Pacific Northwest. I knew the story by heart, because I owned a well-thumbed copy of *The Jewitt Narrative,* having picked up a beautiful numbered edition for a pittance in an antiquarian bookstore on Pender Street. I'll always remember how jittery the clerk had been as I flipped through the spotless pages hunting for a clue to the ridiculously low price. I found it, but I bought the book anyway. I mean, for fifteen bucks, I would have been a superstitious fool to pass on it because it was copy number 666.

It happened in March 1803 (the column began). The American trading ship *Boston* had dropped anchor in Nootka Sound, on the west coast of Vancouver Island. Macuina and other chiefs paddled out from their village at nearby Friendly Cove. They welcomed the Americans and brought gifts of salmon. In return, the ship's captain, John Salter, presented the chief with a double-barrelled fowling piece.

The next day, Macuina boarded the ship with nine pair of ducks he'd killed but pointed out the gun was bad—*peshak!*—because one of the locks had broken. The captain, incensed by the criticism, called the chief a liar and many other names. Macuina left the ship visibly upset and returned the next day with a large party of men. They were unarmed and extremely friendly. At some point Macuina, wearing a hideous wooden mask, blew a whistle. It was the signal. The natives turned on the crew, picking up axes and seizing the stunned sailors' own jackknives then slitting their throats.

A twenty-year-old Englishman named John Jewitt was the ship's armourer. During the attack, Jewitt had been knocked senseless and lay in steerage. After he came to, the hatch opened and Macuina, who had learned a few words of English from previous traders, ordered him above deck.

You gotta pity the kid, even after two hundred years, for what he had to look at.

The Nootka warriors stood facing him, soaked in blood. The quarterdeck was soaked in blood. Twenty-five severed heads were lined up in a row. Each head was brought to Jewitt to identify. Some were too badly mangled to recognize. The warriors clamoured for Jewitt's head as well, but Macuina wanted him kept alive as his personal weapons maker. A middle-aged American seaman named John Thompson, who had been hiding in the ship's hold, was also spared, due to Jewitt's intervention.

Jewitt and Thompson lived as Macuina's slaves for almost two and a half years, finally escaping on the brig *Lydia*, also out of Boston. At one point Macuina told young Jewitt the reason for the massacre. It had been about revenge. In years past, a Spanish captain named Martinez had murdered four Nootka chiefs, including the beloved Callicum. Soon after, the English captain of the *Sea-Otter*, a brute named Hanna, had ordered his gunners to open fire on the canoes tied up alongside the ship. More than twenty Nootkas had been killed, including several chiefs. Macuina had survived by diving off the *Sea-Otter's* quarterdeck and swimming a safe distance underwater. Hanna ordered the attack, the whale king told Jewitt, in reprisal for one of the natives stealing a chisel from the ship's carpenter.

When Captain Salter rudely berated Macuina for damaging the fowling piece, all the old fury over those past atrocities boiled to the surface. So those hapless Americans aboard the good ship *Boston* were marked for unjust and bloody retribution—murder of innocents begetting the murder of innocents being, alas, the way of this wicked world.

Grey day finally came.

Twenty-Six

I'd just stepped out of the shower at seven fifteen when the phone rang.

It was Staff-Sgt. Brennan, speaking in his dryly official mode. "I'm calling to request you attend the Witka detachment this morning to provide a statement," he said. "If that isn't convenient, I can send a member out there to conduct the interview within the hour."

I pictured the panting Shih Tzu sitting on Brennan's desk, the old Scot standing at ease, stroking his thin black mustache in wee patriotic flourishes.

But it wasn't that.

Jerome Charlie had walked into the Witka reserve cemetery last night and shot himself in the head with a high-powered hunting rifle. I was one of the last people to talk to him.

I told Brennan I would be leaving shortly and would go directly there.

"Very well," he said and hung up.

I was almost out the door when the phone rang again. It was Helen, Jake's wife. Jake had got the call about Jerome Charlie almost an hour ago from the district manager of the Department of Indian and Northern Affairs. It was a blow to Jake, she said, because he had known Jerome since high school; when Jake was an electrical contractor, they had worked at the mill together for long periods; and as an MP he'd acted as the federal liaison in the self-government talks.

"I can see he's really down in the dumps, Pat," Helen said.

"Would you mind coming by and maybe try to cheer him up a little? Jake always says, 'Pat Ross, he's the last of just one of the guys.' It's nonsensical, but it tells you what he thinks of you."

I said I'd be right over. The dead could wait, I thought, and so could the Mounties.

It was still coming down steady, so I wore my green raincoat and put on my black snap-brim fedora. I hustled across the wet grass to the Jacobson house.

Helen gave me a small, grateful smile at the door and told me Jake was downstairs in the rec room. I found him tinkering with an old shortwave radio set he'd picked up at a garage sale. Helen and Jake were big garage sale people.

"Hi, pardner," he said.

"Howdy, Jake. Still working on that relic?"

"It's a lot of fun. When I was a kid, my dad used to have one of these, and we'd listen to the news at night. This guy would come on and say something like, 'To all the men and women in the service posted abroad and to all the ships at sea—' I always remember that: 'To all the ships at sea.' I'm going to get this old baby humming and see if I can find an overseas broadcast that still says that."

"Try tuning in a Liberian or Panamanian station."

He laughed at the quip. "Want coffee?"

"Better not. I have to get into town. The RCMP want me to give a statement. I talked to Jerome Charlie yesterday."

He nodded gravely, pulling his mouth down at the corners.

"It's really too bad about Jerome," I said.

Helen yelled from the top of the stairs. "Want coffee, Pat?"

"I'm fine, thanks, Helen," I called back.

Jake sat back in his chair and vigorously rubbed his temples. He looked frazzled. "Jerome got bitter," he said. "I don't think he could face the signing ceremony this weekend, but he couldn't be a no-show either. This was his way out, I guess."

"Jake, did you ever hear about a Witka man named Ezra Paul hanging himself on Settlers Road? It was way back—1949."

"I was just two years old in forty-nine, pardner, so that's a little before my time. I never heard anyone mention it."

"The Barlows really ran the place back in those days, didn't they?"

"You can say that again. They owned almost all of the real estate. Dad landed here after he got out of the service, and he said it was a builder's paradise. Lots being cleared, cabins, subdivisions, public buildings going up like an assembly line. He did most of the wiring. The place was booming like that right into the sixties."

"Anything special about the Settlers Road area?"

"You wouldn't know it now, but that was where the village was back in the garden market days. The Coast then was just a big unincorporated district, and it made sense to have the commercial and administrative centre close to the ferry landing. Once they put in the four-lane highway, and everyone had cars, everything shifted to Witka."

"And the main reserve in the old days was at Hidden Cove?"

"That's right. The band started filtering down to the new reserve as the town grew. They'd always had that strip of beachfront; the Catholic church was there, the graveyard, a few shacks. Jerome's grandfather was the first chief to make the move to the new reserve, and most of the band went with him. They built it up from the ground. It made sense, because the town had stores and schools and a good hospital. The cove was isolated. No school, no services; there was one general store there in those days, and that was it."

"Roy Barlow's about your age, isn't he?"

"Couple years older."

"How well do you know him?"

"He's blue blood. Private schools, summers in Europe. The Jacobsons are more wiener and bean stock. Besides, he and I go to different churches." He raised his eyebrows meaningfully.

"So Jerome would've had nothing to do with him?"

"Funny enough, that's not so. Their grandfathers were very chummy, by all accounts. Things were getting done in those days, and the old-timers worked together. The Barlows and the Charlies were movers and shakers in their separate spheres, and sometimes those spheres overlapped. Their children and grandchildren played in the same sandbox, believe it or not. Jerome also attended Roy's church, if I'm not mistaken. No, Roy and Jerome were friends."

"Even after Jerome set the band in competition with the Barlows?"

Jake chortled. "You could have something there. His church is Roy's castle, but money is his god. I really don't know how things were between them these last few years."

Jake got up and sauntered over to the window in a lazy arc. "Look at that," he said, yawning.

I took a look. It was old Irving, out in his garden, rain or no rain, almost invisible under his big hooded yellow poncho as he knelt down and checked his beloved vegetables.

"He doesn't give up," I said. "I'll say hi to him on my way out, but I better be off."

We took it slow up the stairs.

"Thanks for coming by, pardner," Jake said. "I have an appetite again. Think I'll go have a stack of flapjacks, if I can talk my charming and lovely into making them."

"That sounds pretty good. Tell Helen I'll take a rain check."

"I better be careful, though," Jake said at the door, looking around outside with mock paranoia in his eyes. "That's two politicians who got spanked at the polls, both gone in less than a week. I don't know if I can afford to lose the next election."

Gallows humour. He felt better.

I hailed Irving, then shook my head mournfully when I had his attention.

"This is nothing," he said, turning his neck stiffly in the raingear. "In France, we were out in worse than this for days on end. And we had bullets flying at us, too. I'll take rain over bullets, wouldn't you?"

"Sure, Irving, but there's no war on."

"There's always a war on. Did you try those new potatoes yet?"

"No, I'll get to them tonight."

"Do eat them. You won't taste a nicer, mealier potato all year."

"I will."

Sniffing the air, he added with imperious kindness, "Might come by tonight with a few fresh parsnips."

I knew better than to argue with the oldest soldier on the Coast.

I dashed to my car.

VIII: Rain
Following Jerome
Twenty-Seven

I picked up a rain-soaked faerie couple hitching a ride into Witka. He was a lanky, ashen-faced dude and she was a strapping black woman, truly built. She was shaved bald and prominently pierced. He was wearing the makeup.

They started murmuring to each other in the back, but I felt like talking off topic, and Irving had put me in an English mood.

"Ever hear T.Rex?" I asked.

They hadn't.

"You guys don't know Marc Bolan, eh? Bolan was the original faerie, the futuristic faerie who conquered rock and roll, and you faeries have never even heard of him. Here." I passed them *The Slider* CD case, while I played "Telegram Sam", its high glam pledge of allegiance to the United States.

"Bolan's only known in North America for 'Get It On (Bang a Gong)' and the album it's from, *Electric Warrior*. But in the rest of the world, he was the next big thing after the Beatles, at least for a couple of years he was. He's the edge Brit pop's had ever since, from Bowie to U2. Died young, right before his thirtieth birthday, and a month to the day after

Elvis. Bolan put out some junk, but he also kept recording great songs until the end. He was a prophet and seer, too. Listen to this." I played them "The Avengers (Superbad)".

Over the long metal funk fade-out I said, "He did that in 1974, on his album *Zinc Alloy and the Hidden Riders of Tomorrow,* but did you hear the lyrics? The first and repeated last verse sounded meaningless when the record came out, but the words actually make sense after the 9/11 terrorist attack, what, more than a quarter of a century later.

"'Superbad tiger'—that's Osama, the big cat—'runnin' with your brain.' Well, yeah. He got ahold of everybody's brain. 'Tucked beneath your arms like a devil train. When the angels from the heavens meet the angels from the earth'— those are the victims, on the air and on the ground—'you'll hide inside your cave, uh-huh, that's right, of course.' Of course. 'And we know, we ain't slow, we're the avengers.' That would be the coalition, I suppose. Bush certainly ain't slow.

"The middle verse is pure sexual Zionism—Bolan was also the original sexual Zionist. But I don't know if that's of interest to you faerie folk."

I looked over my shoulder at the woman. "That groovy chick, by the way, chanting 'Dig this' was the mother of his child. Her name was Gloria Jones. She looked a bit like you."

I played "I Love to Boogie" next. "Wild, huh? Yeah, when that should have been a hit over here, we were listening instead to garbage like 'Don't Go Breaking My Heart' by Elton John and Kiki Dee. Can you imagine that?"

In the mirror, I saw they were both shaking their heads in happy disbelief. As my son Clay had said, while downloading the electric boogie opus that stretched from "Ride A White Swan" to "Twenty-First Century Stance", Marc's music lived because it was so full of joy.

I dropped them on Cowrie Street. They thanked me and called me sir, then the guy ran back and asked what the best Bolan album was, so I just handed him the *T.Rex* CD case. "Start with that," I said.

If all else failed, maybe I'd make it with the faeries.

Twenty-Eight

Brennan kept me waiting on a wet plastic chair in the front, where motorists reported fender-benders and citizens lodged complaints to a woman constable through a small steel mesh talking hole in a shatterproof window— just like buying tickets at the movies. Clearly, I was not in the detachment commander's good graces.

A woman in a green tracksuit who identified herself as Mrs. Hutty was telling the constable about her husband's run-in with a plainclothes officer in John Biddle Park. She was very angry about it. Her husband, who was authorized by Health Canada to smoke weed under the medicinal marijuana program, had been walking in the park that morning as part of his daily therapy. He'd decided he needed to medicate, and no one was around, so he went off to smoke his joint. "He's under doctor's orders to medicate once an hour to combat his toxic adrenaline levels," Mrs. Hutty explained.

So he was medicating by a tree, and a guy came out of the bush and grabbed the joint right out of his hand, and crushed it in the earth. "What are you doing?" the husband moaned. "That's my medicine." The interloper explained he was a cop and that it's against the law to smoke pot in a public place, even if you do carry a permit from Health Canada. Then he stalked off.

Mrs. Hutty—a tall, strikingly dapper blonde who spoke with a Yankee twang—said she'd arrived soon after and found her husband looking sick as a mule. He'd told her his sad tale, and she'd blown her top. She got him home to his stash and came right down to the station to set the cops straight. "You can't do that," she told the constable. "It's like taking insulin away from a diabetic."

The constable—a beefed-up, heavy-freckled plain rider in her twenties—excused herself, went back in the direction of Brennan's office and returned a little later to say that the officer in the park had confirmed her version of the incident, but that as far as the RCMP was concerned, he had acted in accordance with the law. "You people are sadly misinformed," Mrs. Hutty seethed. The constable said that until they got written authorization from Health Canada saying permit-holders could smoke their weed in public, that's how the law would be interpreted. Mrs. Hutty promised they would hear from Health Canada within the hour and stormed out.

After she was gone, Brennan and about six other members came streaming out of the back to watch the woman get into her car and drive off. They were all grinning, except Brennan, who looked somewhat mystified.

"What a firebrand," he said. "How does that jellywrist rate a piece of tail like that?"

The woman constable, still sitting at her post, answered smartly, "Have you seen his house in the Gorge? Prime. And to sweeten the pot, if you'll pardon the pun, he's got a super state-of-the-art grow-op—all perfectly legal. For some girls, that would be ample."

Brennan looked down at her, aghast. "Not you, I hope."

The constable shrugged noncommittally, and they all had a good belly laugh.

Ah, the boys of the law.

Brennan kept me waiting another twenty minutes. Finally he came out, glanced my way, muttered to the constable, "Might as well send him in," and went back to his office.

The constable buzzed me into the inner sanctum.

This time Brennan took notes, and I answered the questions.

I told him about my visit the previous day with Jerome Charlie and his angry admission that Sloan had been to see him Friday to grill him about the Ezra Paul suicide. I went over my brief conversation with Jerome, including his reaction when I'd asked him what was going on at the hatchery. Then I told Brennan that I later spoke to a source at Hidden Cove who said there was no such person as Ezra Paul. I related what Esther Henry had said about the Paul family, and how the subject of Ezra was not considered a healthy one to raise among the nation, especially around the Charlies.

The trouble began when he asked me the name of my source.

"A trusted old-timer," I said, "who spoke on condition of anonymity. It's just hearsay opinion anyway, on the source's part, though I believe the source. But surely you guys can find some Witka elders who would tell you whether Ezra Paul really existed. Jerome's wife would probably know too."

Brennan was incredulous. "As if we would put her through that. You don't get it, do you? This Ezra Paul business is ancient history; it has no meaning today, except maybe as part of some two-bit newspaper story that a dead doper was working on. But going around asking questions about events like these—things you know nothing about—can dredge up bad memories and bad feelings for folks who *do* know. Seems to me that all you did was get Jerome really upset. I agree one hundred per cent with what he told you. You've been pressing people's buttons. Picking up from where your old boss left off. Didn't I tell you to leave that Ezra Paul business alone? Now Jerome Charlie's dead."

"I don't think that's fair."

"I don't care what you think."

"Are you sure he shot himself with his own rifle?"

"Get out of here," he said. "I'll get a member to go out to your place next week and take a formal statement if we need one. I can't stand the sight of you; I want you out of here."

I started to go, but he called me back. "Don't go *anywhere* near that reserve. The whole community is mourning a huge loss right now. You show up there, and I can't guarantee your safety."

"I wasn't planning to go there."

"Good. Because I wouldn't endanger one of my members to save your sorry hide."

As I was walking out, I saw the woman constable standing at the fax machine reading an incoming, when her jaw fell open.

"Staff-Sgt. Brennan," she yelped. "Look at *this.*"

Brennan strode over and snatched the page out of her hand. "'From the office of the Director General of Health Canada,'" he read. "Says Mr. Hutty and any other authorized medicinal marijuana permit-holder can smoke—" he looked around at his brother officers who had assembled, "wherever they damn well please."

While the other Mounties dolefully shook their heads, Brennan looked at his watch. "Didn't even take her forty-five minutes. Where do you find a woman like that?"

I waited for the constable to come to the front and buzz me out. She took her time then gave me an upholstered just-try-me look. Tom's girl all the way.

Twenty-Nine

The faeries were looking better every minute. Rita Champion-Davis greeted me warmly in the front lobby of the *Chronicle* building. She asked me what had happened to my face, and I told her I fell on some rocks. From her sour look, I figured that she knew what had happened because Jan had told her. I craned my neck and saw that Jan was on the phone in her office.

Rita said, "Pat, what am I supposed to do about this mad Max character?"

"Max Riverton?"

"Who else? I'm sure he's called at least three times this morning. 'Get a camera down to Dundee Bay,' he demands. 'Make it fast. They just pulled up in another truck.' What a nutbar he is."

"Maybe you should check it out."

"I won't talk to the man. He's a complete babbling idiot."

A customer walked in and asked to speak to the editor. Rita skipped around the counter and said she was the editor; what could she do for him. He was a stocky middle-aged guy in a Mackinaw, fairly intelligent looking. "You wrote this story," he said, holding up a folded newspaper. Rita stared at the type. "It has your name on it," he said.

"Yes, I wrote it," she said quickly. "What about it?"

"You refer here—" he pointed to a line "—to an accident involving a semi-truck."

"Yes?"

He fed her back the silence. Then he said, "The word 'semi' means one-half. I have yet to see a one-half *truck*." Rita shifted her bulk from one foot to the other.

He spoke to her as if to a child. "The part that has the motor and driver is called many things: cab, rig, tractor, truck. The part that carries the cargo is called the trailer, if at both ends it sits on its own wheels. If the back end sits on its own wheels, and the front end sits on the tractor, then it is called a semi-trailer. Got that?"

Rita smiled outwardly. "Yes. Thank you."

"There is a semi-trailer, but there is no semi-truck."

"Right. Got it."

"Good. In case any of your reporters are confused, I've put it in writing." He passed her a sheet of paper with a few lines typed on it. "Keep it around as an easy reference."

Rita took the paper. She was still smiling, but her face was cherry red. "Thank you again, sir."

"Dennis," he said. "I'm not asking you to print a correction. Just to correct yourselves. Have a pleasant day."

After Dennis left the building, Rita spun on her heels, crumpled the paper and hurled it at a wastebasket, missing. "*You* have a pleasant day, dumbass," she fumed, stomping off to her desk.

"What was that about?" Jan said. She had finished in the office and was standing next to me, putting on her blue raincoat.

"Fellow named Dennis was trying to educate Rita on the definition of semi-trailer," I said, as we went out into the rain.

"Did he succeed?"

"I don't think so. She was too angry to listen."

"Did you know the proper definition?"

"Semi-trailer? Well, hell yeah. I used to drive one."

We ate lunch at the Harbour View Inn, both of us ordering catch of the day soups and Greek salads.

Jan had really pulled herself together since I first saw her Sunday night; it seemed as if keeping the paper going, Albert's paper, was keeping her going. In her dark tweed jacket and skirt outfit and crisp white blouse, she was the perfect image of a capable, confident publisher. If you looked closer, though, you'd notice the haunted eyes, the pale trembling hands.

"Unbelievable about the chief," she said.

"What do we know about it?"

"He left his house sometime between midnight and one in the morning. His wife didn't hear him leave. He took his deer-hunting rifle. Apparently walked over to the cemetery— no one saw him, but it's just like a block away. Sat down on a bench overlooking the sea, not far from his parents' headstones, and pulled the trigger."

"Did he leave a suicide note?"

"We don't know. The only reason we know anything is because Shawna lives down there and saw the emergency vehicles arrive. She talked to one of the paramedics. I guess someone heard the shot and called it in." Shawna was a typesetter at the *Chronicle*, a white girl married to a reserve man.

"And the RCMP are definitely treating it as suicide?"

"Foul play not suspected," she said, as the waitress brought our soup and salads.

We ate in quiet then she asked, "What did you find out yesterday?"

I told her about the Ezra Paul mystery. Her expression was interested but subdued. I also told her what Brennan had said about digging up the past, and how it might have affected Jerome.

"I've thought about that, too," she said.

"Having second thoughts, Jan?"

She considered the question, very calmly, her teeth clenched under her closed lips. Then, with eyes lowered, she nodded. "I've had to get real honest with myself, Pat. I realize now that Albert and I weren't very close those last months. What you said to me yesterday morning, about Albert possibly being disturbed or unbalanced, it could be that he was, but he was keeping it from me, and I was choosing to ignore it. I mean, look at that bonsai tree. What was that? Was that a sane act?"

"Doesn't appear to be, in light of what happened. Do you think the big story was just a false front?"

"I know he was genuinely excited after talking to Virgil Wood, especially one time when he went to see him in the hospital. But whatever secret he thought he could uncover, I think it might have died with that old man."

"So you want me to bail?"

She covered her eyes with one long hand and sat like that for a full minute, head bowed, taking occasional deep breaths. Then she dropped the hand and looked straight at me.

"Where else can you go?" she said.

I thought of Big Bill, but I couldn't tell her about Big Bill. So I said: "Barlow. He's the one who knows. Whatever Virgil Wood knew, Barlow knows."

"I'm sure Roy knows a lot of local secrets. But other than abducting him and carrying him off to the woods, then maybe torturing him with a hot stick, how do you expect to get him to tell you anything?"

"I could always join his congregation."

"What?"

"That's a joke. They wouldn't take me. No, your point is valid. But I would like to try to talk to him one more time. A couple of other loose ends, too, I wouldn't mind tying up."

The waitress brought the bill, and Jan picked it up. She turned to me with a brittle smile.

"Well, I brought you in, even if I was crazy with grief at the time. And you were good enough to do what you've done. So stay with it as long as you need to. Tomorrow I've got to bury my husband. We'll have to fill the next edition with tributes to Jerome Charlie. It's starting to feel like too much grief, too much death. Let's just try not to hurt anyone else, Pat, okay?"

I left the tip.

Thirty

I parked in front of Barlow Enterprises and tried to collect my wits. As a close friend of Jerome Charlie's, even if they had become business rivals of sorts, Roy was probably spending the day at home, mourning the loss of his pal. He might even be with the Charlie family on the reserve, although I couldn't really picture that. Maybe they were all at church together. Or maybe, since money was reportedly his god, Roy was a hundred feet away inside his swank office in the Barlow Block. It would be easy enough to find out.

I got out of the car and had taken a few steps in that direction when I heard a voice from the past sing out: "Patty! Patty!"

It was Salim Marwari, the *Vancouver Star*'s ace blood and gore guy, standing outside the mall entrance in a belted knee-length beige leather coat, a big, wicked smile playing on his lips.

Salim had a soft cherub face, but it was misleading. He was a powerful man, at least six-three, and could handle himself if a crime scene he worked turned hot. An Ismaili Muslim from Tanzania, Salim had been shipped to England for his education back in the seventies, when Idi Amin was chasing ethnic Indians like Salim out of Africa. He gloried in recollections of swinging London and the Fleet Street tabs and spoke in a rich, relaxed baritone that freed interview subjects from their natural inhibitions against talking to strange reporters, especially foreign ones.

"So this is where Patty lives," he intoned, arms outstretched to the horizons. We shook hands and went into the mall for coffee.

In the food court, he sized me up. "You look like a tree fell over on you. I thought you were the great white wood chopper."

"I got waylaid by some goons in the bush. What are you doing here?"

"They sent me up to link the two suicides. Can't ignore the suicide angle when you've got two somebodies like this back to back. 'Death comes to paradise'. Isn't that beautiful, Patty? These weren't kids on sniff. What's going on up here?"

"Not sure yet."

"Are you working on it?"

"I'm asking around."

"Not for this bloody little hick town rag? Come *on,* Patty. That's kid's stuff. You were doing that before you even got laid."

"Maybe I've come full circle. But it's probably not for publication, Salim."

His eyes grew shrewd. "You're saving it for a book? Hey, you knew Sloan—you must know a lot about what's going on."

I stirred my coffee.

Hunching towards me, he put on his patented glare of wonderment. "You *know.*"

I shook my head. "Not enough to put anything together."

He finally gave up on the evil eye routine and sat back, casually surveying the food court for noteworthy customers, hot babes in particular, though he was a devoted family man and supremely loyal to his lovely wife. "These suicides, you know, often trigger copycats. Individuals who are prone to it seem to draw resolve from other people who take the plunge first. There's a window of inopportunity, so to speak. Did the old chief know Sloan very well?"

"They weren't friendly, but they knew each other."

"Were they at odds?"

"Yes. Hit the *Chronicle* back files to last spring's band

elections, when Jerome Charlie was defeated. Read the run-up. Sloan was after his scalp."

Salim scratched his jaw. "That's interesting. So they were old enemies. Joined together in death."

I had to laugh. "Yeah, something like that."

"And they both lost the last elections."

"Less than two months apart."

"This place is hard on losers."

"Who have you talked to so far?"

"I just got here. But I did some phoners from the newsroom before I left. The cops, the new chief, some pols."

"Get anything?"

"Just crap. They're all saying crap. Family tragedy, community needs time to heal, self-government will be Chief Charlie's lasting legacy to his people. Crap. No one wants to put up any explanation as to how paradise went rotten for these guys. They're just worried about the bloody tourists and not offending the Indians."

"Well, dig up some of that *Chronicle* stuff. Play up that bitter-rivals-meet-their-end angle. You can tell them I sent you. That is, if you can bring yourself to walk into a hick-town rag. Remember, though, the lady running it now lost her husband just a few days ago. She might give you a few words, but go easy."

Salim nodded at my suggestion. "You're right, Patty. That's the best angle. And I'll go easy on your girlfriend." He winked at me.

Outside, he made one last pitch. "Come on, Patty. Tell me one right question to ask."

"Figure out your own right questions, you lazy sot."

He gave me a friendly shove. "You're just saving it for the book."

I wrote down his cell number in case I thought of the right

question and pointed him toward the *Chronicle* building.

I walked back to the car, rolled down my window to let in a little rain, and smoked a cigarette.

I could sense that Salim wasn't thrilled about the assignment. He was trying, but he knew this wouldn't be a hot talker that would get him into the front five with a nice key on the cover. Too close to feature or column material; not enough juice for a hard news hound like Salim. No bad guys, just dead guys. And what was I really holding back from him? Precious little. What we had were two failed politicians, aging men whose egos had finally caught up with them. Even Jan saw it. She'd brought me in, yes, but now she was ready to move on. And I didn't want to let go. I was clinging to some lame hope of finding meaning where none was to be found. Pat Ross, another failed player; a failure at life, trying to prove that he was still part of it, when in fact he'd left it behind with his sad and sorry marriage and his own collapsed ego. Maybe Brennan was right. My visit might have helped drive Jerome Charlie over the edge. Ripped open an old family wound that was no one else's business, certainly not mine. *What was I thinking?*

I was ready to pack it in when Harry Shimizu pulled up in a white pick-up with Sayonara Gardens emblazoned on the side in leafy green script. He got out of the truck and walked determinedly toward the Barlow Block, but checked himself within a few feet of the doors. Nervously, he looked to his left and right. Then he walked in.

I forgot my ennui and waited. A few minutes passed. I had to be sure, so I went into the lobby and asked the woman at reception—not the same one I'd seen Monday—if Mr. Barlow was free at the moment.

"I'm afraid he's got someone with him right now, sir."

"Ah," I said. "Right, I just saw Mr. Shimizu come in."

"Yes, he just got here, so I have no idea how long he'll be in with Mr. B."

"No problem. It can easily wait. I just happened to swing by. Thanks."

I walked out before the receptionist could ask me my name or the nature of my business with Mr. B.

I went back to the car and sat. Almost an hour had passed before a scowling Shimizu exited the building and drove off. The white pick-up led me back to the garden centre on Taylor Road.

IX: Growers Coast

Thirty-One

The alluring redhead was pricing wicker baskets behind the counter; the rain seemed to have washed away the customers. I introduced myself.

She said, "Hi, I'm Ruby Shimizu. If you're here to see my dad, I think he just went into the greenhouse."

I found Harry moving in with his pruning shears on a potted pine tree. Although it wasn't even four o'clock yet, the grey outdoors sent in an autumnal end-of-the-day gloom.

Harry stopped clipping when he saw me. "Yes?" he said.

"Hello, Harry. Remember me from yesterday?"

"Yes, I do. You gave Mrs. Sloan the tree?"

"I did. Seeing it was hard on her, but it helped clear things up a little. I think it was necessary."

He looked briefly puzzled by the remark. "Well, it's hers now. Is there anything else I can do for you?" He was blinking at the potted pine, as if it was important he get back to it.

"I was hoping we could have a talk. There's been some odd happenings, and maybe we can share information, help each other figure things out."

"I have *no* information."

"You just spent an hour talking with Roy Barlow."

Fear and suspicion twisted Harry's face. He shook the cutters at me. "I think you should go!"

"Fine, I will. But hear this. Since Friday, two men have died, apparent suicides, though neither struck me as particularly suicidal. Since Monday, when I started asking questions, I've been beaten up, threatened, warned repeatedly, lied to repeatedly and blamed for one of those deaths. I've also started getting weird phone calls in the middle of the night."

"Hang-up calls?"

I turned around. Ruby was standing behind me in the doorway, a deep furrow creasing her fine brow.

"Yes," I told her. "With Indian drumming music in the background."

"We've been getting those for days, haven't we, Dad? And other things have been happening, too."

Harry cut her off with a sweep of the arm. He spoke to her sternly, as if I wasn't there. "We don't talk to *him* about it. We don't know who he is. It would be foolish to trust him." He ordered her back to the till.

She didn't go. "You're wrong," she said hotly. "*I* know who he is. He's a writer, a newspaper columnist. He's famous. Everyone in Vancouver knows who he is. So do you. Remember last winter when you were reading that series on the salmon farms in the *Chronicle*, saying Mr. Sloan was doing the right thing by exposing them? That wasn't Mr. Sloan. That was Pat Ross—*him*. He wrote all of those stories. If there's one guy we can trust, this is the guy." She went back to the till.

Harry placed the pruning shears on a wooden bench and exhaled deeply. Then he turned, arms akimbo, legs spread, regarding me with a gritty sidelong gaze.

"We'll talk in my office," he said.

It was a dark, cramped room with adding machines, deposit bags, receipt books and other essentials of doing business littering the battered walnut desk. Open boxes of ceramic planters ate up the usable floor space in front of it, so I squeezed into a high-backed wooden chair next to Harry.

"I'm planning to sell," he said. "The business, the house, everything. Take my family back where we belong."

"Where's that, Harry?"

"The Niagara Peninsula. That's our home. Coming here was my first big mistake. Going to Mr. Sloan was the second."

"How come?"

"He thought he was playing a game. He could have avoided all this trouble if he'd just done what I asked him to do."

"What was that?"

Harry sat there thinking, rolling his tongue back and forth inside his cheek. Then he opened a drawer and removed an old four by six black and white photo in a clear plastic protector. He laid it down in front of me.

The setting was familiar. You could see a sliver of the Strait of Georgia and the Island in the background, behind the blossoming cherry trees. It looked like Virgil Wood's property. A date was written at the bottom: April 24, 1926.

It was a group shot. About forty men and women, young and old, more than two dozen children. They appeared to be prosperous farm people, turned out in their Sunday best. A few of the men posed with pipes in hand or their gold watches flicked open. Maybe that's why some of the women were smiling so much. They all looked proud and relaxed, masters of their domain.

They were all Japanese.

"Last summer I took this picture to Mr. Sloan at the *Chronicle*. People told me he was willing to go up against the powers that be, so I decided I would take a chance. I explained it to him. The first Japanese came here before the Barlows or any of the other old families. They built logging camps up in the mountains and laid the corduroy roads that you can still find today, if you go hiking in the bush. The Japanese men were very entrepreneurial. Some of them bought up tracts of land and started clearing it. They brought in livestock, grew fairly large-scale market gardens and planted fruit trees everywhere."

"When did the Barlows enter the picture?"

"All this was going on when John Barlow landed here. His original holdings were very modest, a few acres east of the ferry dock. The white settlers called that area Barlow's Landing, but the place itself in those days was called Growers Coast."

"Growers Coast?"

"Yes, and the Japanese people were the Coast growers. When the Barlows and the other families who came after them were still clearing their land, the Japanese were marketing their produce in the city. They operated the early ferry system. My great-grandfather built a slaughter plant; the family ran it for decades. In 1898, Ujo Hara opened a jam factory on Lower Road. He was very successful, like a lumber baron almost. That picture you see was taken on Hara Farms, just below Ujo Hara's house."

I thought of the turreted original structure of Virgil Wood's home; the rose bushes and monkey puzzle trees; the fishponds; the arbutus bridge.

"Hara Farms was enormous," Harry said. "It started somewhere on this side of Settlers Road and took in at least seven, eight miles of the shoreline."

"I live on Hara Farms," I said absently.

"This was a Japanese Canadian economic centre for close to half a century, but it was isolated and that's what the old Issei wanted. There was truly obscene racism in those days, all up and down the whole West Coast. Union types formed their anti-Asian leagues and went on rampages. One time in

Vancouver, mobs completely destroyed Chinatown. They rioted on Powell Street, too, but the Japanese fought them off. It was different on the Growers Coast. Here the *hakujin* were the newcomers. They were in the minority for a long time, and they accepted that because there were many benefits. They had a really nice setup. The village was called Akita, named after a town in northern Japan some of our people came from. They had local government, good stores, a couple restaurants, a pretty little schoolhouse, even a movie theatre. They even had a public pool. There was segregation in the city, but not here. Everyone got along okay. Then the war came."

"Oh, no," I said.

"Oh, yes. The government took everything. Right after Pearl Harbour, as I'm sure you know, Japanese Canadians—twenty-two thousand of them in B.C.—were stripped of their property and possessions and herded off to detention camps. Concentration camps. First the RCMP came over and registered and fingerprinted everyone. Then they sent them to the bloody fairgrounds on Hastings Street. Put 'em up in the livestock building, which stank to high heaven, and tried to civilize them by feeding them baloney and milk. That went on for months. Then they shipped them all inland to the camps.

"During the war, the old white families on the peninsula bought up everything for nickels. The same thing happened all over. The big berry farms in the Fraser Valley, the fishing fleets in Steveston, blocks and blocks of Powell Street, too. Sold off for peanuts. The difference was, hardly anybody knew about this area. Our people weren't political. They were just farmers, and they'd gone out of their way to keep this place off the map. So the Barlows and the rest capitalized on this. When they took over, they rubbed out every trace of the Japanese. Maybe they thought it would be bad for business if people knew. They certainly made piles of money. Subdivided all the land into cottage lots and sold them like hotcakes. They even abandoned the old village and replaced it with Witka, twenty miles north."

"That's when they got the natives to move down there from Hidden Cove. It helped legitimize the switch," I added.

"Sure, there was nothing up there then. Time was on their side, you see. Even after the war was over, the government passed a law preventing JCs—Japanese Canadians—from returning to the Pacific coast for almost four more years."

"I didn't know that."

"Oh, yes. It wasn't until 1949—March 31, 1949—that we were allowed to come back. They had a good seven years to erase us. And what was there to come back to anyway? Everything had been stolen. They said my father resisted—they almost deported him to Japan, though he was born here. But he resisted because he didn't like them taking away our land and our dignity, and he told them so. For that he was sent to a POW camp in Ontario. The rest of the family joined him there, and we eventually settled just outside St. Catharines. We've all done rather well. My brother has a successful vineyard, my cousins and nephews and nieces are all professionals. We work hard. We're not lazy people. When we had to start fresh, with nothing but the shirts on our backs, we did. *Shigata ga nai,* my mom used to say. It can't be helped.

"But some of the Nisei wanted to come back to their birthplace, start over again on the West Coast. Joseph Hara, Ujo's son, was one of them. Joseph had fought in the First World War. For *Canada*. He was a war hero. Medals, everything. He came to visit us when I was a very small boy. I remember my mom and dad thought he was a great man. And I have this image of him as this very exuberant tough guy. But he really had no one. His parents were gone. His wife died in the camps. His two teenage girls were his only family. He worked in the beet farms in Manitoba at first—they sent some of the people there—but after the war he started logging and doing teamster work in northern Ontario. Over the years he built up quite a nest egg. The spring of 1949 was when he came to visit us. He gave my parents some money and asked them to take care of his daughters while he got himself established out west. Those girls became older sisters to me. But they never heard from him again.

"My sisters and I always wondered what happened to their dad. That was one of the reasons I came back—to see if I could find out. But I also wanted the people here to learn the truth. That this was a Japanese Canadian place before it was anything else. Their hard work made it what it is today. The peninsula was an untouched wilderness. Then our people came and poured their blood and bones into it. They deserve some recognition for that."

Thirty-Two

So what did Sloan say when you told him all this?"

"At first he thought I was crazy. He knew the local history, and there was no mention of Japanese people, except for fleeting references to the logging camps. I said of course. That's because the histories were written according to the selective memories of the pioneer families, who didn't want posterity to remember the Japanese. He was on council then and checked land titles, but he said there was no record of the family names I provided owning anything. The records were either destroyed, I told him, or they were altered. He wanted to see our redress documents from the federal government, so I showed him. But they only listed our holdings in acres and buildings and gave "B.C. Coast" as the location. That's it. That's all we have. He said he would look into it some more, but then I didn't hear from him for many months. During the springtime, he started coming back, asking further questions. I said why don't you just run the picture, let me tell my story, and maybe others would come forward. But he didn't want to do it that way. He said he'd found a source, someone local who might be able to confirm a lot of what I was saying, but that he had to get this person to open up to him."

"That would be Virgil Wood, the poet. The late poet."

"I didn't like the way he was sitting on everything. He seemed to be getting more information, because now he was acting more like he believed me, and he would ask me very specific questions, but he would never tell me what he found out at his end. He acted like it was his story now, not mine. That his telling it was more important than us having lived it."

"A lot of reporters act that way. I didn't think Sloan would."

"During the last month or so, he came back several times. He kept saying he was 'almost ready to spring it'—those were his words. 'Don't lose that picture,' he'd say. 'It won't just be front page on the Coast; it'll be front page from coast to coast to coast.' But I didn't really believe him. I'd stopped trusting him. He had me working on that replica bonsai for his missus, and I thought he'd gone maybe a little—you know—upstairs."

"No, I think he *was* ready to spring it," I said. "Do you mind if I have a smoke?"

"Go ahead." He set an ashtray in front of me and placed the photograph back in the drawer. "But if my daughter sees it or smells it, she'll be mad."

"No, she thinks I'm great." I took a long drag, dreading what was to come.

"From the looks of things," I said, "Sloan was ready to tell his wife the story. He was a ham actor, big into theatrical productions, and even as a politician and newspaperman, he liked to show then tell. He was going to hand over that little bonsai tree then tell his wife the story, the whole story. The tree was part of it."

Harry frowned like he blinked, with his whole face. "How is that?"

"What Sloan learned was that a man had hanged himself in that tree in April of 1949. Early April."

Harry's face sort of seized up.

"I'm sorry," I said. "But it does sound like it was Joseph Hara. In the *Chronicle* morgue, Sloan dug up a newspaper article from that year which described the death. The article said the dead man was a Witka native. I checked into that, and it seems that there was no such person. They invented an Indian to explain Joseph's corpse. Awful, huh?"

Harry was staring straight ahead at the wall. A wildlife calendar showed some kind of small lizard. "Outrageous," he muttered. His head swung around. "But that's ludicrous. How could he know it was that very tree?"

"There's a gash in the trunk. You can still see the mark if you go down there and look at it. The article said the man started to chop down the tree then gave up and hanged himself from it. It also said he was drunk on cheap whisky at the time. Does that sound like the way Joseph Hara would have ended it?"

Harry shook his head, his mouth puckered in rage. "No, not him. I bet they killed him," he said.

"They might have. In those days lynchings were supposed to be confined to the Deep South. But they all listened to the same Bing Crosby songs. Why did you go to Barlow's today?"

"My family's frightened. We've been getting those strange calls. They wake my wife and daughter up at night. They don't say anything; just that drumming and high-pitched wailing and then they hang up. One morning there was a dead fish sitting on the hood of my truck. The next morning it was a dead seagull. Looked like it was shot with a pellet gun. One of our cats has disappeared."

"Whereabouts do you live?"

"In town, near the Gorge. Right below Barlow's big castle. I told him about all the stuff that's been happening. He said we had a prankster on our street. Even said it might be an old boyfriend of Ruby's doing it. I told him that was not true. I reminded him how his father had made the family fortune: buying up confiscated Japanese Canadian lands at fire sale prices. He acted like he didn't know what I was talking about. Said he wasn't privy to all his father's and grandfather's land deals. That they did things different in those days. Oh, he was ready for me. He had land title records in his desk drawer. Pulled them out and flashed them. See, he said, see. I said we have our own records. Up here." He tapped his skull. "And in here." He slapped his chest.

"Then he really pissed me off by saying the federal government had compensated us a few years back, and how many times did we want to be compensated. I told him that he couldn't buy me off; that the truth would come out. I wanted to call him a thief from a family of stinking thieves, but I held my tongue. I'm afraid I said too much as it was. I have to think of my family's safety first."

"Of course you do. Have you gone to the RCMP to report the threats? Because they sound like threats."

"To say what? To say a fish landed on my truck? They'll say it dropped out of a bird's beak. To say that a bird landed on my truck? They'll say a neighbour's kid shot it out of the air. To say my cat is missing? They'd laugh at that and say I should never have let him out. To say the Barlows are land thieves and maybe killers? They'd probably lock me up for that."

"I see your point."

"Will you write my story?"

"I might have to," I said, getting up. "Sad truth of the matter is, though, that it doesn't feel like it's over yet. I'm going to try to fill in a few blanks. I'll be in touch."

We shook hands.

At the counter, I gave Ruby my home phone number and told her to call if anything else happened, no matter how seemingly innocuous. I also thanked her for stepping up to the plate for me.

"We have to trust someone," she said.

"Yes, but I think you've filled your quota for this month. Go easy now."

Thirty-Three

On Lower Road, I slowed down at Virgil Wood's house and saw the turrets through the rainswept trees. I parked in the next driveway over. There were lights on in the house, so somebody was home. I used the brass knocker.

Big Bill came to the door, wearing a black apron over a combat fatigue jacket and baggy grey sweatpants. "U.S. Army" was stitched on the shoulder of the rolled-up jacket sleeves. He had a gun in his hand, the kind bakers use to decorate cakes.

"What the hell do *you* want?"

"I've just come from talking to Harry Shimizu. I think I've put most of it together, but I'm still wondering exactly how Virgil fit into the picture."

Big Bill started to close the door. "Well, he's dead, so why don't you go ask him?"

"Even without Virgil, I bet I know more than you do." The door stopped about two inches away from the jamb. "I know what Albert learned those last few weeks, after he cut you out of the fun and games."

The door swung back open. "What has that skanky bitch been telling you?"

"People on Settlers Road saw you and Albert together, hanging out in the apple grove. Then they saw Albert hanging out alone. I did the math," I lied.

"These people who saw me, how do they know it was me?"

"They described you. I know it was you."

"Did you tell the fuzz?"

"No, I didn't."

"Why the hell not?"

"I had no reason to."

He let me in.

It was nice inside, kind of macho New Age. Incense and bearskins. Big flat-screen TV in one corner, Pure Land Buddha niche in the other, lots of comfy but not flashy expensive furniture in between. Oversize frameless blowups on the wall, with Big Bill in Nepal, Big Bill in Peru, Big Bill under Kilimanjaro. Always posing with the local little people. Big Bill's karmic safari.

"You can wait in here if you want and watch some tube," Bill muttered, "or come with me into the kitchen. I'm just finishing something."

I followed him into the king-size kitchen.

Eight pies were lined up on the bright countertop. Each was identically stacked with symmetrical rows of overlapping glazed mandarin orange slices. On the six pies that were finished, lines of delicately swirled fresh whipped cream ran between the mandarin rows, with a fat application of cream circling each pie's outer edge as well. The unfinished pair exposed the surface of dark amber filling beneath the slices.

"I'm doing my creamy mandarin orange pie recipe," Big Bill said. "I'm taking a couple over to Kewp's as a peace offering tonight. Excuse me a minute." With his decorator gun, he squeezed whipped cream on the two unfinished masterpieces. "There." He tossed the tool loudly into the sink, sucked the cream off his large freckled thumb and flicked the switch on a deluxe Braun coffeemaker. Then he carved up a pie. We each got a quarter.

It was on par with what you would get in one of the finest European bakeries in the city.

"That is some crust," I raved. "And the filling is like a very light custard. What's that flavour?"

"It's an orange liqueur. 'Nother piece?"

"Better not."

"We can do in that one; there's seven left."

"No, I can't eat half a pie for supper. But that was really good. Thanks."

He poured coffee, and we each lit a cigarette to have with it. Using a sandalled foot, Bill pushed open the sliding glass door a few inches to let in some wild sea air.

"So you talked to the Japanese dude."

"Yeah, and I broke the news that it was probably his stepsisters' dad who swung from that tree fifty-five years ago."

"Albert never told him?"

"Nope."

"What a jerk. He held everything back from everyone. That was his problem."

"Shimizu said the same thing."

"So what did Albert find out before the end?"

"Why don't you start at the beginning, then I chime in at the end? Avoid backtracking and repetition."

"You're a clever dude. Even after you eat my pie, you want me to go first."

"I can do dishes after if you like."

"Funny. I met Albert at Kewp's a year or so ago. Back in March or April, we were talking one day, and I told him my neighbour's backyard looked like a Japanese fandango. He asked who it was, and I told him Virgil Wood, the poet. He'd heard of Virgil. I think he interviewed him once a long time ago and read some of his books. He said he would be interested to see the yard, so I took him over there, and I guess the two writers got reacquainted. Albert started going over all the time. Sometimes I would come over, and the three of us would smoke a little bud."

"The three of you?"

"Yeah, ninety-year-old poet liked his reefer. Said they used to do it on the beach once in a while back in the '30s then stare at Hieronymous Bosch paintings in a book. They were like pre-beatniks, I suppose. I noticed that Albert used to wait till Virgil got buzzed, then he'd start pumping the old man about the property. Who built the bridge? Who planted the trees? Who gathered up the fresh kelp? The old man would give him some inscrutable answer, then go up to the attic and bring him down a couple pages of verse to take home. I thought it was some kind of cryptic dharma shit they were doing together. But I could see Albert was really into it, and the old man would tense up quite a bit during these bull sessions.

"One day Virgil came over to my place—it was one of the first truly summery days we had in May—and we got into some imported beer. The old guy was a lot of fun, he really was. That day I put it to him: what the hell were he and Albert always going on about? So he told me. He told me about the Japanese getting here first, clearing and planting everything, that they were basically running the show when he'd arrived on the scene as a beach bum. And he told me how the Barlows and their buddies snapped up all the confiscated lands; how everyone on the Coast sort of got amnesia about who the true pioneers were, and how the Japanese in general got royally ripped off. He told me all this, but he said not to tell Albert, because Albert was a conniving s.o.b. and always put his own interests first. He also said there were still people on the Coast who didn't want the secret to get out, and that they wouldn't think twice about ruining someone or worse to keep it safe. You know, the family values crowd. So I kept my mouth shut.

"Then in June, the old guy got sick, and they moved him into the hospital. I went up there with Albert a couple times to visit. One time in the car, he started saying he should go in alone first, so he could get the old man to talk freely about his writing techniques, or some shit like that. I told him to cut the crap; that I knew what he was trying to get out of Virgil and that Virgil didn't trust him with that kind of information. It was funny, because that bit of news didn't seem to offend or faze Albert in the least. He just shifted gears on a dime. He said if Virgil was being forthcoming with me, then I had to find out what he needed to know. Then we would both know, he said, and we could both profit from that knowledge."

"Profit?"

"That was the word he used."

"What did he mean?"

"Didn't explain it—just threw it out there. But he told me what he wanted to know. He said he needed to find out what happened to this Joseph Hara dude when he came back to the Coast. I didn't know what he was talking about, so he filled me in on Hara Farms and the fact that Virgil was living in the guy's house, and that we were all basically legal squatters on the guy's land.

"Poor Virgil. I remember going up there that night. He had tubes up his nose, and he looked like he was on his last legs and knew it. He'd never see his precious fishponds again. I asked him about Hara, and he said Hara had come back and hung himself in the apple grove on Settlers Road. He called him the soldier. He said the soldier came back and never left. That he was still here, which really creeped me out."

"So you told Albert, and the two of you went out there."

"Yeah, just scoped out the place. He filled me in a bit more about Hara. How—after he got out of their fucking camps—

he pinched pennies for years as a lumberjack and whatnot so he could get his ass back to the garden. Then I guess he got back to the garden and saw how the greedy white devils had cashed in. Must have been pretty devastated to off himself."

"If he did. The good old boys might have done it for him."

Big Bill tightened his jaw. "Is that what Albert found out?"

"I don't think he had that—it'd be pretty hard to get at this late date—but he must have suspected it. How could anyone not suspect it? Anyway, that was Shimizu's first reaction."

"See, that freaks me out when I hear that. In a way, I was glad I didn't talk to Albert after that day we went to Settlers Road. I saw him at Virgil's funeral a couple weeks later, but we didn't sit anywhere near each other. I had bad vibes about the whole thing and wanted to just forget it. We all have our secrets. Places have their secrets too. Sometimes it's better to just leave it at that. Still, I didn't like the way Albert used me then factored me out of the equation."

"He did get more. He dug through old newspapers and found a story about the hanging."

"Really?"

I told him about the Ezra Paul deception.

"So the Indians were used for the cover-up," he said.

"There's more." I told him that the story identified the actual tree, and that it was the same tree Albert was found hanging from.

Big Bill went pale. He lit another cigarette. "That's too much," he said. "Who did he tell this to?"

"He went to Jerome Charlie with it."

"Yeah? Is the old chief admitting that?"

I looked at him. "He's not admitting anything now. Didn't you hear?"

"Hear what?"

"Jerome Charlie shot himself in the head last night in the Witka cemetery."

"No fucking way."

"Yes fucking way. The other person he told it to, I'd say, was Roy Barlow."

"And then he died."

"And then he died."

"Have you been to see Barlow?"

"I went there Monday, but I had nothing to throw at him. I've got plenty now."

Big Bill got up. "I don't mean to be rude, you seem to be a pretty nice guy. But I want your fucking car out of my driveway now. And you better be in it."

I got up to leave.

"And please," he said, "don't come back."

I nodded as I passed the Pure Land Buddha.

X: A Killing on Cowrie Street

Thirty-Four

Cowrie Street was a zoo, and it didn't take long to see why. The Mounties had yellow-taped an entire block of the commercial strip.

I parked my car in the Bank of Montreal lot and walked to the south end of the perimeter, where a herd of onlookers was pressing up against the tape, and the two RCMP cruiser cars were positioned diagonally to help secure the cordon.

At the other end, I could see a similar herd gathered.

All eyes were drawn to the west side of the block, about halfway up, where the police had taped off a perimeter in front of the Venture-West offices. I counted nine police and emergency vehicles parked chaotically in front.

"What happened?" I asked a couple of older lady gawkers. They didn't really know. Someone had got shot.

I moved through the packed crowd and spotted a logging contractor I'd interviewed once over some labour trouble he'd had. "What's going on, Doug?"

"From the sound of it, Max Riverton brought his duck hunting gun to town. Went in there and took out Lars Lovedahl." Doug turned to his companion; they were both wearing red and white old timers league hockey jackets with different numbers on the back. "Wonder if Max had that thing registered?" They both chuckled.

"So is Lovedahl dead?" I asked.

"The ambulance didn't leave in much of a hurry, I'll tell you that."

"What about Riverton?"

"They got him. He didn't put up a fight. Lady at the craft store said he just laid the gun against the wall and waited for the sirens. Guess he got tired of looking out on galvanized steel fish pens."

Doug's friend muttered something to him. "Oh, yeah?" Doug said. He turned to me. "Bernie says they just put four more pens in Dundee Bay this morning, and Lovedahl was on site when they did the assembly and floated them in."

Lovedahl's last caper.

I found Salim, the big-city reporter, leaning against a cruiser car in his long belted beige leather coat, his back to the crime scene. He was talking on his cell but ended the call when he saw me.

"More trouble in paradise, Patty." He was keeping up a cool, sombre front, but I could see he was inwardly bursting with excitement. He had a real story now and a solid three hours to file for first.

"Who is this Max guy?"

As I told him what I knew about Max, Salim hauled out his notepad and wrote down the things he liked. "Max was the main reason the industry came under scrutiny last year and why there's a moratorium on new farms. Max lives on Dundee Bay. One morning he wakes up, and his downward ocean view is taken over by a mess of galvanized pipe, a floating dock, Caterpillars and pre-fab huts on the shore, and workers in raingear with feedbags. Residents had no forewarning. A company back in Norway, some buddies of Lars, barged the stuff in during the night. So Max phoned the media and became the voice of lost equity outrage; he owned a hot waterfront property that had been hit by manmade, government-sanctioned lightning. But the media campaign was maybe too successful for Max. The moratorium satisfied the public, but it meant operators had to limit their activities to existing sites—like Dundee Bay. And that's what it sounds like happened."

"What about this Lars Lovedahl?"

I told him about Lovedahl, too. "Brought the aquaculture boom to the Coast, everyone acknowledges that. Hired as a development officer for the municipality but was let go because all his energies were spent growing the fish farms. He was candidly a hungry man on a merchant mission. There had been talk lately about a disease outbreak running through the farms, and Lovedahl was linked to a possible cover-up. Max knew about it for well over a week, so it looks like his rampage here is tied to what happened just today down at his place. I can't offer you a single source other than Max for the outbreak rumour."

"I won't touch it."

"I wouldn't."

"So this will be a big setback for the aquaculture industry on the Coast," he mused aloud, obviously not thrilled with the sidebar possibilities.

"Look up the name Werner Veitch in the phone book." I spelled it. "He's listed. He lives at Dundee Bay, a few houses over from Max. He's the caretaker there for Joni Mitchell. It's her house."

"Joni Mitchell: that's great."

"The desk will like it a lot better than 'Fish farm industry reeling.'"

"Bloody right. But too bad it couldn't be that chick from No Doubt. Or even Chrissie Hynde. I've always wanted to make that voice talk back to me."

"Well, Joni's the best I got. I don't think she'll do an interview, but Werner might be able to get a statement from her. Something about how violence doesn't solve anything, I would think."

I could see that Salim didn't much like the sound of that.

Thirty-Five

The Mounties were holding a presser for eight o'clock that evening. We took a short cut between buildings to the detachment headquarters.

TV and radio crews were already setting up and testing inside the media briefing room. The *Vancouver Sun* had its Coast stringer there; Rita had sent a summer student to cover the murder for the *Chronicle*. I quizzed the kid and learned he was handling both reporter and shooter duties—even crime scene shots, for which he had no glass to strap onto the ancient, warped newsroom Minolta he was wearing around his neck. It ticked me off. Never mind that this was the juiciest news story of the summer, or that the staffer who'd have to follow it through the justice quagmire was far better served getting in from go. Like part-time Bartlebys, the *Chronicle* bunch preferred not to work nights.

Brennan came out with a prepared statement. At 5:07 p.m., the RCMP Witka detachment had responded to a report of shots fired on the four hundred block of Cowrie Street. Members of the detachment arrived at the Venture-West offices at 5:16 and discovered a male, age forty-one, deceased. Identity withheld pending notification of next of kin overseas. A male, age forty-seven, was taken into custody at the scene.

"Homicide charges are expected to be laid within twenty-four hours," Brennan said, "but until that time no further information will be released."

Salim turned to me dumbfounded and said, "Can they do that? Give nothing?"

"That's what they do. But on the bright side, the less these other guys get, the better."

He grinned and winked at me then threw a question at Brennan. "You said shots were fired. How many were fired and how many hits were there, to the best of your knowledge?"

"Those details are part of the ongoing homicide investigation."

The *Sun* reporter, a thoughtful, corpulent man with lank blond hair, asked if police believed the shooting was related to frictions that had developed on the Coast between residents and salmon farmers.

"It would be premature and inappropriate to draw any such link or ascribe any motive whatsoever at this stage of the investigation," Brennan said. "Of course," he added, looking at me, "there are elements in the community that have been agitating against the aquaculture industry, and the premises where the shooting occurred are manifestly associated with that industry. If there is any connection established, we will thoroughly explore those dimensions as part of our investigation."

"What, is he Dr. Who?" Salim whispered, but the *Sun* reporter was getting it all down.

A young woman reporter from one of the TV stations piped up next. "Staff-Sgt. Brennan, this shooting is the third violent death on the Witka Peninsula in less than a week. While we recognize that foul play has been ruled out in the other two deaths, both involving well-known members of the community, is there anything you can say about the unusual grouping of these deaths and what impact it might have on the public here?"

Brennan squirmed. "I don't really follow your question, I'm afraid. We look at each case individually, and to speculate on how the public is affected by violent acts committed in their midst is not the role of law enforcement; it's more in the realm of social science or psychiatry. What we can inform the public in this latest case, which is the only one in which a crime can be said to have been committed, is that there is no need for alarm or concern about personal safety. There is no danger posed to the public. An individual is in custody. Charges are expected to be laid within twenty-four hours."

"So the individual in custody is a suspect—*the* suspect—in the homicide?" one of the radio guys said, innocently enough.

"I didn't say that," Brennan scolded. "*You* said that. I think I was very clear in what I said. Well, that's all for tonight, folks. We will issue a release tomorrow to all newsrooms informing your editors and producers of the time of the next scheduled press conference. Good night, everyone. Thank you very much, all of you, for coming."

Salim shook his head as Brennan strode away. "How to complicate simple murder," he said. "Why not at least admit the guy's the suspect? I talked to a dozen people on the street, and they all knew what happened. The only unknown was how many slugs he pumped into the Norwegian. Why obfuscate like that?"

"To make your job harder," I said. "Of course, Max is the suspect, and there's no reason why victim and shooter—alleged shooter—can't be identified tonight. That business about overseas next of kin is pure malarkey. But why say anything, if they don't have to? Now you have to source all of that hearsay you picked up on the street, and if you get one little factoid wrong, they'll be right down your throat. If you get something major wrong, or just print something that they don't want to see out there, they might blacklist your news organization. That's how they chill the story."

"Bonehead approach, guys," Salim said, his eyes showing

more sadness than anger. "They're just locking out potential witnesses, Patty. The important ones, who might step forward in the critical first twenty-four hours. Someone who could prove premeditation. Plus, they're upping the odds that the public does wind up getting fed a dose of crap."

"But the likelier scenario is the public simply goes hungry. The RCMP doesn't believe, as a matter of policy, in the public's right to know. They would prefer it if the public didn't know a crime was even committed. They say it's all about protecting the integrity of their case. But it's really so they can operate with minimum public scrutiny. Lawbreakers are their meat; the public is their enemy. That's the Mountie mindset."

"Makes those mouthy bastards at the Vancouver PD look pretty good after all."

Salim went off to call Joni Mitchell's caretaker.

Thirty-Six

I'd driven into town for two reasons. (1) To buy a slab of fresh fish. (2) To drive up to Roy Barlow's Gospel Rock estate, talk my way in and broadside him with a news flash.

On both counts, I changed my mind.

My news flash for Barlow was going to be a bluff. I was going to let him know that I had decided to write the Growers Coast story and had successfully pitched it to an editor back east, e-mailing all my notes, contacts, phone numbers, everything—so that if something did happen to me, the editor would easily be able to assign the story to another writer. One way or another, it was getting out. The purpose of my visit would be a magnanimous one. I was going to give Barlow a chance to give his side of the story. "No point in denying it, Roy," I'd say. "I've got enough documentation to bring it home without you."

Problem was, I didn't. Not yet. Nevertheless, I figured that by going to him like that, there was a fifty-fifty chance he would play ball. And even if he didn't, at least he would think that the secret was now out in the open, and that national print had it. Yes, I was looking for insurance. Because, like Big Bill, I now considered Barlow an extremely dangerous man.

I decided instead not to bluff. I could get the story. Shimizu could feed me the names of the other displaced families. I could track down a handful, bring in the Japanese Canadian Association—or whatever they called themselves, because I knew there had to be one—and talk to some history profs at UBC and Simon Fraser who were steeped in the confiscation and internment saga. Sell the experts on the plausibility of Harry's story, make them want to pursue it, report the fact that they intended to, and pick off the quotes of conditional outrage. I could do, in short, what Albert should have done a year ago. Feature Harry prominently, and use his powerful photograph. Barlow's silence would be nothing less than a sinful admission. I could do it all, working the phone, in two, three days.

Do it, I thought. Just do it.

On the highway, I stopped at Baldur's Meats and bought a twelve dollar porterhouse steak.

No, sir. I wasn't fooling around.

XI: Ruby and the Night

Thirty-Seven

I was trimming the fat off the steak when the phone rang. It was Ruby Shimizu. "Have I got you at a bad time?" she said.

"No, not at all."

"I'm at the garden centre, and I'll be closing up in ten minutes or so. Dad had to drive to the ferry terminal to pick Mom up; she's coming in on the 9:15 boat. I feel silly calling you."

"Why?"

"Well, you said to call if something happens, but nothing's happened. That's just it. There's no one here. Just me and the wind and the rain. This place, out in the middle of nowhere—I guess I'm a little spooked."

"I don't blame you, with what's been going on. This place is spooky at the best of times. Tell you what. Have you eaten?"

"I had some noodles a few hours ago."

"Okay. You just won the lottery, honey. I'm going to leave here in one minute. I'll drive to Sayonara Gardens, and you lock up and bail when I get there. You can come back to my place, and I'll cook you a nice supper. How's that?"

"I like it."

"Better call your dad."

"He doesn't have a cell."

"Smart man. Was he planning to drive back there to pick you up?"

"No, they're going straight home. I've got my car here."

"Call home then, leave a message, tell them where you're going to be, and give them my number."

"Am I being stupid?"

"Who cares? We'll see you in a bit."

I brought Ruby back to the cabin and cooked us supper. Even halved, the steak was too much, but it was good. With Irving's new potatoes, a few steamed parsnips (they were hanging from the doorknob in a plastic grocery bag when Ruby and I got back to the shack), a little tossed salad (with Irving's own butter lettuce as the foundation), and some good red Bordeaux I'd stashed away for just such an occasion, we ate well, drank well and became quite merry—and fairly frank.

Ruby was twenty-nine and had a journalism degree from Carleton University in Ottawa. No wonder she'd inflated my credentials. Instead of working in the industry, she'd moved out to B.C. to help her parents get established. She had a boyfriend in the city—a shipping agent with an office in the Marine Building—but she suspected he was being unfaithful to her. She wasn't sure about her future. She loved B.C. but agreed with her dad that the family would be better off going back to St. Catharines. The Coast had turned out to be a nightmare. She didn't know if it was time to separate from her parents and perhaps start her own life in Vancouver, or return home with them and enter the journalism field in the central Canadian heartland.

"There's certainly a lot more opportunity there," I said. "More dailies, national print."

"I'm thinking electronic."

"TV? You'd be good. I haven't seen your copy, but Carleton isn't known for turning out slaggards. You're smart. You enunciate well. You're very nice looking."

"Oh, I'm not. I'm short, small in the chest, I've got a big butt, big thighs, huge ankles and fat calves. And I've got a horsey face."

"Ruby, you're mistaken. You're a classic beauty."

"I am not."

"You are. The long willowy ones are nice, sure, but the earth goddess build is still the universal standard. Mass culture has tried to convince us otherwise, but to no avail. Not if we listen to our hearts and groins."

I went over to the bookshelf and came back with a photo in a gold frame: a three-by-four black and white of a woman leaning against the wooden hull of a beached fishing boat.

"You see that woman? That's my estranged wife, Caroline. She was built just like you. She's a little less curvaceous now—after about forty, I think, body types change some—but she's still an earth goddess. She's beautiful."

"She has a very lovely, wise face."

"So do you. You're what my mom used to call a prize package, my dear. If this shipping agent doesn't see it, he's a prize chump. And make no mistake, you would go over big on TV."

I told her about the TV reporter and her question at the Mountie presser. "It was a very good question," I said. "A lot of print people look down their noses at TV folk, but they shouldn't. TV has fabulous reach and great potential, but you have to capture that moment in real time, that single soundbite moment. You really have to learn to set it up. That gal made a valiant try."

Ruby asked about the Lars Lovedahl shooting. I told her what I knew. "What's going on here?" she said. "It's turning into a death trap. I keep wondering who's going to be next."

She said her father was deeply hurt to learn the likely fate of Joseph Hara. "My aunts will be devastated when they hear. Dad doesn't want to tell them over the phone. I don't blame him."

"Maybe they should come out here and see their heritage. It is theirs."

"It might be too hurtful. When something is yours but people say it isn't, that's almost worse than having nothing."

I pulled out the box of Virgil Wood's writings. It was amazing what a difference a few days had made. Some of the verse fragments now screamed with meaning.

One was called "The Known Warrior".

The bridge he built stands sturdy:
There was rapture in his toil.
Now the known warrior comes at night,
Carrying his lethal coil.

"Wow," said Ruby. "That's Joseph."

"Virgil actually reads that in the TV documentary. He was reciting it to school kids for Remembrance Day, wearing a poppy. Went right past me when I heard it on the video."

We found another fragment about "pirates raiding the ship that sailed under the crimson sun/Stranding the radiant crew ashore then making their blackguard run."

There was even a verse he started called "Akita General Store", which began: "I buy wonderful fruits of the sea at Akita General Store."

We watched the CBC video, *Milk From the Mountains.*

The real giveaway came near the end, and I'd missed it altogether. First Virgil spoke about "ancient Witka ways forgotten," but then he shifted into a whispered, *"And then came* the earth builders, the ghosts in yonder hills." When he said "shrines of the disinherited," the camera was panning the Hara cherry trees in full blossom. The poet was trying to tell the truth, but the truth wasn't a matter of great importance, it seemed.

I piled the Virgil Wood material back in the box and carted it away to my office. From the living room, Ruby asked if I had any more wine.

"I've got a passable Beaujolais, but I better not join you. I'm going to have to drive you back to town sometime tonight."

"You can join me," Ruby said. "I can crash here."

"What will your folks think about that?"

"I'm almost thirty. They know I'm not a virgin."

I didn't ask what she was getting at. But I did fill both our glasses.

As I was sipping on mine, Ruby looked up in alarm. "Did you just hear something?" she said.

"No."

"I thought I did."

We looked out the windows but couldn't see anything except a porch light burning at the surgeon's and the fruit trees shivering in the night drizzle.

"Maybe a raccoon," I said.

We sat down again in the living room, but this time Ruby sat close to me on the sofa.

"Ruby, when did you guys start getting those weird phone calls?"

"The first one was Saturday night. Then another one Sunday, and I think Tuesday."

"So they started after Albert's death."

"All the creepy stuff started on the weekend. That's when we last saw Milky, our beautiful white cat. I can't believe he's gone. And those calls—I've taken all of them. Those wailing voices sound like demons or something."

"What I heard sounded like the drumming that always accompanies the traditional winter dances. There's nothing demonic about them. I even participated in one once, years ago."

"Really?"

"It's all about taking a journey into the lower world. The traveller visualizes a deep hole in the earth and enters it. He goes along a passage until he arrives in the lower world. There he encounters spirit beings. What the drumming does somehow brings clarity to the visualizations. Makes the dream pictures vivid."

"Did you make it to the lower world?"

"I did. I came to this wild underground cavern that looked like something right out of Jules Verne's *Journey to the Centre of the Earth*. I sat astride a giant bird that flew me to a rock ledge, and there was a bear standing upright on the ledge. I got off the bird and went with the bear."

"Wow. And you saw all this?"

"As clearly as I see you. It was like I was there. I couldn't tell you what it meant, though. I assumed they were my guardian spirits, but you have to keep doing it before you start learning things down there that you can bring back with you."

"Why did you stop then?"

I laughed. "Maybe I did find it a wee bit demonic. I wasn't thrown by the experience itself; it was quite invigorating. I remember afterwards, though, a local Buddhist whitebeard was quite worried about me when I told him about it. He said the fact that I encountered animal beings meant I was operating on a very unevolved level, spiritually. Mind you, he and I disagree on a few things. No, I think like a lot of people around here: I delve into something, but when it starts to get real, I find a reason to delve out."

"That's fascinating, though." Ruby topped up our wine glasses. "I have noticed that a lot of people up here seem to be into esoteric ideas."

"Oh, this place is the capital of esoterica. Just about everyone up here is into something. Crystals. Numbers. Past life readings. Nude dream workshops."

"Come *on.*"

"I kid you not. What else? Aquarian horoscopes, they're still doing those. Aliens, of course. There's a landing base around here. Sasquatches in season. Whatever the tide brings in. What else? Some people up here won't even eat breakfast before consulting their Tarot."

"Oh yeah."

"I have a Ryder deck. It's in that cabinet next to you, wrapped in a silky orange cloth. Haven't pulled it out in years. I used to like the Number 19 card, the Sun."

Ruby brought out the bundle and set it on the coffee table, slowly unfolding the cloth.

"Cut the deck and see what comes up."

She turned up the Number 12 card, the Hanged Man.

"Oh no," she said.

"That's pretty bad," I admitted. "That's why I don't like messing with that stuff."

"What does it mean?"

"I'd rather not speculate. You're supposed to interpret the cards positively. I'm pretty sure this one means that you're in a suspended state, going through some troubles that should be character building in the end. But with all the stuff that's been happening around here, I don't know what it means."

Ruby stood up and said, "Now I'm really scared." She looked it, too.

In one swift motion, she covered the two stacks of cards

with the tail of the orange cloth and swung around onto my lap, hugging me tight.

I could feel her eyelashes moving against my neck. Then she really put some muscle into her hug. "Poor angel," I said, holding her as gently as I could.

She drew back her head so that we were facing each other. Her chestnut-brown eyes were sober and fierce but her mouth arched down as if in utter despair.

I gave her my best rendition of her brash crooked smile.

With a soft intake of breath Ruby gave me back the real thing. Slowly she took my chin in her fingertips and kissed me.

Following the kiss, we looked at each other for a long time, matching expressions of doubt, amusement, ease.

Presently she said, "Why don't we go lie down."

While Ruby was in the bathroom getting ready, someone knocked on the door.

I opened up, and Harry Shimizu was standing on the porch in a wrinkled beige raincoat. He looked tired and grim.

"It's after two," he said. "I've come to drive Ruby home."

As Ruby stepped out of the bathroom, I said, "Ruby, your dad's here to pick you up."

Looking a trifle stunned, she came to the door and peered out. "Oh, hi Dad," she said.

She turned to me and murmured flatly, "I guess I'd better be off."

Harry walked back up the slope to his pickup.

Ruby gave me another one of her hard hugs, said "sorry about this," then sat down to tie her sneakers. In a chipper tone, she rated the meal and conversation the best she'd had since leaving Ontario.

I said, "Who the hell in Ontario could top either?"

"I'll have to think about that one."

In the doorway I said, "Tell your dad I'll be calling him tomorrow for some contact numbers. I've decided to take a crack at writing his story."

Ruby gave me a warm smile from the porch. "He'll be glad to hear that."

I watched them drive off. Now that was a tough break.

Thirty-Eight

I was sleep-deprived from the night before, but I still wasn't tired. Energy is energy, even bad energy, I guess. I felt hungry again, so I put together a little snack. I found a beer in the back of the fridge, a Harp lager, tagged it for later, and refilled my wine glass. Then I sat back to drink, smoke and think. The first two were easy.

I thought of how sweet it was to become slave to a woman's body, face and mind. How lovely Ruby was. How ready I was. How lucky I wasn't. How it was all for the best. How I didn't really believe that. How there would never be another time. How there might be.

I got off that kick and started brooding next over the surreal events in Witka that evening. I winced, recalling the way I'd so bitterly condemned the Mounties to Salim. Whenever I torqued the truth like that, there was always something personal behind it. I knew I was furious at Brennan for suggesting my ten-minute visit to the carving shed had helped drive Jerome Charlie to suicide—he even had me believing it for a while (but it wasn't true, was it?)—then implying at the presser that "elements" (such as I) might have had a hand in nudging Max Riverton to go out and murder Lars Lovedahl in cold blood. But there was still more to my anger than that. Finally, I had a pretty solid handle on the background leading up to Sloan's death, but Brennan's closed, confrontational attitude had made it impossible for me to go to him with what I'd learned. Now, with the murder on Cowrie Street in their laps, and the Vancouver media in their faces, the Mounties were right out of the game. That left me standing in the crosshairs.

I thought about Max and his rage. We all knew he was obsessed to an unhealthy degree over the salmon farmers' incursion into his postcard-perfect world; he talked about his plunging property values with more hand-wringing despair than chemo patients talking about their cancer. But I saw a lot of that on the Coast. It was as if the urge to be close to Mother Nature and ardently protect her from the vile mechanical world, had brought out the rankest materialism in some people. Max had then just taken it to the extreme.

And poor Lars. He loved nature, too. He had a nice acreage high up on the slopes, raised bighorn sheep in his pasture. Had a good-looking wife, small children. I'd met them all once when he'd driven me up there to see his spread. Kids came running out to greet him. Freckly little tots like their mom with peaches and cream complexions.

Just a guy trying to look out for his own and make his million the only way he knew how. I wondered whether the family would bury him here or ship him back to the fjords of his native Norway. Then I realized, with some dread, that it was already Friday, the day of Sloan's funeral.

There was a knock on the door.

I felt a thrill as I went to answer it, thinking Ruby had ditched the old man and made it back for that lie-down.

Big Bill towered in the doorway.

Thirty-Nine

He walked in, followed by a strange man and woman who looked like they'd just stepped off the Greyhound from Thunder Bay.

But I didn't really bother to notice the couple. I was looking at Bill. He was different. Maybe he was coked up. He stood in the kitchen as if he'd been a regular visitor and smiled at me with his thin, curled lips showing beneath the trimmed whiskers. It was a mean smile, and his small lead-coloured eyes were somewhere else. He spoke in an oddly quiet voice. He said, "That was real choice whip you got me. I want you to pick up some more."

He handed me a folded twenty-dollar bill.

I looked at him, perplexed. "What the hell are you talking about?"

His hard face showed no anger. The cold, forced smile was still there. "The place is bone dry, and that was just excellent whip you sold me last time. I want a little more." As I hadn't taken his money, he placed the folded bill on the edge of the counter.

I picked it up and handed it back. "I don't know what you're thinking or trying to pull, but I don't want your money, Bill, and I can't get any whip for you."

Bill didn't take his money back but said something so low I couldn't even hear him. In answer to my annoyed, puzzled expression, he drew my shirt collar slowly together and lifted me almost off the floor, till our faces were inches apart. His power was considerable. The smile was gone. His voice remained quiet, but now I could hear him. "I've had my eye on that redhead from the garden centre. I saw her in here with you when I came by earlier tonight. She's got a real exciting little ass."

Panic had risen in me and was growing into sheer terror, but nothing moved. I thought of using arms or legs, but somehow I couldn't. He had me.

He continued to speak, very calmly, holding me aloft. "Kewp told you all about my business, and you're running around shooting your mouth off, swapping secrets with everyone, including cops. Tonight I brought witnesses to the fact that you're a seller. If the cops come around, they'll tell the cops what we did here tonight. And the cops will find the whip, because it's here, believe me."

Bill lowered me to the floor and bent over for a last soft-spoken word. "You don't know who I am. If I want that redhead, I can have her. If I want you buried deep in the bush, I can have that, too. No one will ever know what became of you, or her."

The cruel, disengaged smile came back. A little louder, he said conversationally, "Call me when you get it. Make sure it's that good stuff that you got me last time."

The three of them left.

I sat shaking in the kitchen. After a few minutes, I went outside and grabbed the axe. I returned to my spot, propping the axe against the wall, within reach.

That seemed to help. At least the shaking stopped.

Forty

Iwas washing my face in the bathroom when I heard a knock on the door.

"Who is it?" I called out from the other side.

"Just me, pardner."

I let Jake in. He showed concern as soon as he saw me.

"Everything all right?" he said. "You look a little shaken up."

"It's been a pretty crummy night."

Jake pulled a mickey of Crown Royal out of his brown trench coat pocket. "Maybe you could use a slug."

He came in and sat down in the living room.

I don't like whisky, and I'd finished off the second bottle of wine, so I didn't need any more to drink; but to be polite, I brought two glasses with ice into the room and poured myself a last one.

"I've got a Harp in the fridge. We could split it for a chaser, if you want."

"Naw, this is good," Jake said, taking a small taste.

I sat back and did the same.

"Rain's stopped," Jake said. "Clearing up nice out there."

"That's good news. You're sure up late. It's almost four thirty."

"Couldn't sleep. I was trying to catch updates on the Lars Lovedahl shooting, but they didn't have much."

I told him what I knew.

"Bad business," he said. "So how is the research going?"

"Fair. I've picked up a little bit more. But I think I might just drop the whole thing."

"Really?"

"Jan is tired of it. She's getting past the denial stage, I guess. Time to move on."

"That's too bad. I was hoping you'd dig up some interesting Coast history. Never did find out what Sloan was working on, eh?"

I shook my head. "Not really."

He got up with his glass and went into the kitchen. I could hear the tap running. "You bullshitter," he said, and laughed.

He came back to the living room without the glass and sat hunched forward on the sofa with his legs spread wide apart, his big tradesman hands dangling limp in between. The leer on his face was simian. "You were with the Jap for almost two hours today. His daughter was over here tonight playing tiddlywinks with you. After leaving the Jap's, you went straight over to the doper's house next to Dink Wood's barn. You were there for over an hour talking to him. I see he came back tonight, too. What have you got?"

His upper lip folded belligerently. *"What have you got?"*

I studied the man. Jungle face Jake.

He laughed and looked away. "Good stuff." He screwed the cap on his micky and slipped it into the pocket of his coat, which he'd folded over the sofa arm. His hand came out with what looked like a snub-nosed .38-calibre pistol. He was pointing it at me when he asked me the third time. "What have you got?"

I told him. He got me to slow down at a couple of places in the story. He wanted to know Shimizu's reaction to the Ezra Paul hoax. I lied, telling him that Harry was just very sad to think that Joseph Hara had taken his life that way. He nodded glumly, as if sharing the sadness. I told him that Big Bill knew very little of the history and wanted to be kept in the dark because he thought the whole thing was bad karma. Jake found that funny.

"They're both afraid of Barlow, but Harry doesn't seem to suspect Albert's death was anything but suicide," I told him.

"But you think different."

"I didn't until a few minutes ago. It didn't seem right; it would never have seemed right, but I wasn't prepared to take that leap."

"Your old boss didn't see it either. That's why he was easy prey. Same as you, chum."

He got up, stretching his whole body, save for his rigid right arm, extended by the length of the gun barrel. Yawning, he stomped his left foot, once.

"Let's take a walk, pardner."

Forty-One

The west wind had scrubbed the sky clear and was blowing fresh off the sea. When I was a kid, my dad used to tell me that wind carried the scent of spices all the way from China. I would gaze across at the Island and imagine I was looking at Japan.

Jake walked close behind me up the wet slope. Twice he pressed the muzzle of the gun against my back, high up. Once he warned, in a high, silly voice he sometimes affected, "Don't try something stupid now."

We passed my car and continued up the steep driveway, between the monolithic cedars. The moon and Venus were the last holdouts in the violet sky of pre-dawn.

About halfway up, Jake said, "Take a right."

There was a path leading into a clearing. We'd been there together before. When I'd first moved up, I'd gone into the bush and chopped down a dead ancient alder. With a big handsaw, I'd started cutting it into sections for firewood. It was a huge task, but I saw it as a therapeutic workout. Jake showed up on the second day with a chainsaw, gave me a head-shaking E for effort, and the two of us had finished the job that afternoon with his power tool.

He told me to stop when I reached the stump of the tree I'd felled. I saw the rope above me. It was lashed to the sturdy bough of an overhanging spruce.

"Hope you don't mind," Jake said. "I borrowed the rope from under your hovel. But it's all yours."

I spun around, and he was right there, pushing the muzzle against my forehead. "I'm not going up there," I said.

"Yes you are, pardner. Or you're taking it right here, right between the eyes. Either way's fine by me. I've diversified."

"You killed Jerome Charlie, too."

"I wouldn't say that. No, I would say that Jerome made me make him kill himself. Just like the other bozo, your old boss."

"And then me, and then who's next? Shimizu?"

Jake seemed to give the question some thought. "I doubt it. He'll turn tail, I think. After you, he won't try to shop that story around again. Besides, he looks kooky. Who would believe a blinky like that? The picture means nothing. Japs on a Sunday picnic; big deal. Now be a good boy and get up there. I've got a funeral to go to. I'll give you five seconds, or I pull the trigger."

Boosting myself up on the waist-level stump reignited the pain in my right leg. I teetered but managed to hold my balance. Jake had backed away but was still pointing that damn pistol. I stood there, waiting for the right moment to jump and make my crippled run through the jungle, probably with a bullet in me.

"Good stuff," Jake said soothingly. "Now all you have to do—"

Behind Jake a voice spoke. "All *you* have to do is drop the gun, Jacobson."

It was Irving's voice. The old man stood at the edge of the clearing. Even in the gloom I could see the liquid discharge from his eyes running thick down his cheeks and dripping from the tip of his nose.

But he had a good grip on the shotgun; it was aimed straight for Jake's head. "I said drop the pistol on the ground, or that's where you'll be."

Jake laughed in that high silly voice and looked up at me. "Can you believe this old fart?"

"This old fart," said Irving, "has been watching you. I've seen you with your Mr. Hyde face on, sneaking off at night to do your killing."

The word triggered the action. Jake swung his arm toward Irving, and I heard the loud blast.

Birds freaked out in all the trees, as the air filled with burnt gunpowder smell.

Both barrels had evacuated Jake's head from the ears back, making two holes in front like eyes on a rotted pumpkin.

Irving lowered the shotgun and wiped his face with a hanky folded in his huge hand.

I slid down the stump and crawled around Jake's flat corpse to where the little man was standing. I'd broken down completely and was bawling, hugging his legs.

"You're such a beautiful man," I whimpered.

"There, there." He patted my head. "It was the same in France, with the lads. They could face death all right, but if they made it through somehow, that's when they fell apart. They could face death. It was facing life again that did it to them every time."

XII: Life's Big Holy Terror

Forty-Two

Ithought the truth about what happened had died with Jake. I was wrong. Helen, Jake's wife, knew everything. She told the cops. And Tom Brennan told me.

He came by the cabin that Sunday—a week after Jan had dropped the rattlesnake in my lap—and we drank coffee and ate a couple of plates of my cold fried chicken and warm potato salad while Brennan went slowly through about eighty typed pages of interview notes.

It turned out that Jake didn't give a damn if the whole world found out about the Japanese settling the Coast; it was a Conservative government, after all, under Brian Mulroney, that in the late 1980s had finally got around to paying out twenty-one thousand dollars in redress to each JC survivor. So Jake could score political mileage out of that. Nor did he care about the Barlows and the other descendants of the "nouveau pioneers" destroying old records and newspaper archives to keep the Growers Coast past a secret. The Jacobsons weren't one of the old families; it was nothing to Jake. Even the misreported death of Ezra Paul, in and of itself, wasn't the problem. "In those days," Jake told Helen, "Indians and Japs pretty much looked the same to white folks anyway. Especially when their faces were purple from strangulation." So it could have been a simple case of mistaken identity. An honest mistake. If anyone had any explaining to do about the Ezra Paul hoax, it was the Witka leadership, and they didn't have to explain anything, because they were First Nation and keepers of their own mysteries. Non-natives prying into that would be ethnocentrically out of line.

But behind the Ezra Paul hoax was the murder of Joseph Hara it served to cover up—and keeping that secret drove Jake to commit two fresh murders, and attempt a third, more than half a century later.

Joseph Hara came back to the Coast with about seven thousand dollars saved from working as a teamster and logging contractor in northern Ontario. He called Dick Barlow from a pay phone at the ferry terminal, and Barlow picked him up in his Ford truck and drove him to the old municipal building on Settlers Road, in which Barlow had a land office. Hara had just passed his fifty-second birthday; Barlow was in his late thirties.

Hara was stunned to see that they'd practically cleared the Akita town site. But he told Barlow he would accept the new order on the Coast, and he wanted back in. He was willing to start small—with whatever land he could purchase with the money he'd saved. Preferably, he wanted to buy some subdivided parcels of the old Hara Farms, but if none were available, he would take whatever he could get.

Barlow sat him down in his office and told him he couldn't come back. He wouldn't be welcome; his return would only create tensions with the cottage people, who weren't as enlightened on matters of race as the old Barlow's Landing crowd had been. Hell, they were already clashing with the Witkas at the other end of the peninsula. "To these people, Joe, a Jap is a Jap, and we just finished fighting the Japs," he said.

He told him to go back to his own people in Ontario and forget about the Coast.

At first Hara argued. He said his money was good wherever he wanted to spend it, and the law now said he could live anywhere he wanted to in Canada.

His attitude enraged Barlow, who said Hara had better get the idea out of his hard head, because no one on the peninsula was going to sell him a square foot of land.

Hara then stopped arguing. He could see he wouldn't get anywhere with Barlow, so he was probably figuring a way of getting around him. Barlow guessed this and told him that a ferry would be leaving in less than an hour, so he would drive him back to the terminal and see him off. Hara politely declined, saying he was going to visit his parents' gravesite before he left. Barlow said there wasn't any point—the old Japanese cemetery had been in the path of the new highway, and they'd bulldozed right over it. "Remember, we were at war with you guys."

That's when Hara lost it.

He went outside, hauled an axe out of the back of Barlow's truck and crossed the street to the apple grove. Perhaps at that moment, he figured he would chop down every tree his family had planted on the Coast; dismantle paradise. Maybe he was simply taking out on the tree what he wanted to do to Barlow. Later, he must have wished he'd gone back into the building and done it.

He'd only got in a few swings before a public works road crew ran out and tackled him. They bound his hands and ankles and locked him in a closet in the fire hall.

Meanwhile, electrician Fred Jacobson had come by the town office to inquire about a building permit, heard about the ruckus and went upstairs to see Barlow.

Jacobson was a brawny giant, still in his twenties. He'd served in the Pacific Theatre during the war and had an unreserved hate on for the Japanese. Many times growing up, Jake would get to hear how the Japanese army had done cruel, inhuman things to Canadian, American and British boys; really ugly stuff to demoralize the enemy.

Barlow, no doubt realizing he had the right man for the job, recruited Fred Jacobson to go with him to the fire hall next door and try talking some sense into Hara.

Hara sat on the floor in the dark closet, his back against the far wall, eyes lowered. Barlow asked if he was ready to get on the boat and promise never to return.

"You can't make me leave," Hara said.

Barlow tried to explain things then asked again, but the answer was the same.

"You can't make me leave."

It became a drill. The pair would go back about every hour. Same question, same answer. By the third or fourth visit, Fred started lifting Hara off the floor and knocking him around a little. Telling him to show some respect for his betters.

By then the municipal office staff had gone home for the day, and the public works crew had packed it in; it was just the three men. The drill continued into the night, Barlow and Fred taking a break once to grab a meal at a café on the highway.

Between visits, they sat in Barlow's office and discussed different strategies for dealing with Hara, but couldn't hit upon a satisfactory plan.

Barlow, his gloom mounting, said repeatedly, "I tell you, Fred, I don't want him here."

To which Fred would respond, "I don't blame you one bit, Mr. Barlow. Neither do I."

Barlow pulled out a bottle of Scotch, and the two started to drink.

It was after midnight when they went down for the last time. Barlow made his pitch. Hara gave his stock answer. Fred gave Hara a couple of backhands. This time, though, Hara spat in Fred's face.

"No Jap spits in my face," Fred told him.

A coil of rope was hanging from a hook. Fred took it with one hand and, with the other, seized Hara by the rope binding his ankles. He pulled him that way, the older man's back dragging and bumping along the floor, through the empty fire hall, across the road and into the apple grove. There, Fred hanged him.

Barlow stood with him under the tree while they waited for Hara to strangle to death.

Fred said, "It's what the Japs would've done to one of ours for the same offence. You don't spit in a man's face. Not when you're in captivity you don't."

Barlow said, "It was the only way."

The next day, everyone got their stories straight—Clerk Houle and the others were told that Hara had broken free, found a bottle, drunk it and committed suicide.

No one, apart from Dick Barlow and Fred Jacobson, knew who he was. In fact, one of the workers who carried him off to the fire hall had made a remark about the "crazy Indian", so that gave Barlow an idea. He contacted Chief Benjamin Charlie on the new reserve, and together with the chief, he cooked up the Ezra Paul story.

The traditional Indian burial written about in the newspaper account was a fabrication. The corpse, wrapped in blankets, was dumped into the Strait of Georgia from the stern of Barlow's cabin cruiser. Old Chief Benjamin was the only other person on board.

Barlow was generous with everyone involved, including a ne'er-do-well poet who lived in a shack near Barlow's Landing and went around asking a lot of questions afterwards. He had seen Hara riding in Barlow's pick-up truck that day and recognized him from the pre-war years.

Virgil Wood traded his silence for a free acreage of prime waterfront, complete with the home and garden of the forgotten Hara clan.

Barlow awarded Fred Jacobson's electrical contracting business more work than Fred could ever handle; a second thriving company existed almost solely on the jobs Fred turned down. In the early sixties, Barlow backed Fred for a successful run in provincial politics; when Fred died of a heart attack in the late seventies, he was British Columbia's attorney general. Dick himself died in 1994, having retired a decade earlier and passed Barlow Enterprises on to his son Roy.

About twenty-five years after the Hara killing, Roy Barlow and Jake were in their cups at a Kinsmen campout. Their beautiful young wives went for a stroll on the beach, and the two men were sitting alone by the fire for quite a while. Somehow they got talking about the post-war boom years and, eyeing each other warily, they inched closer and closer to that day. At some point, each man knew that the other one knew.

"Dad did what any trained soldier would've done," Jake said. "The little nip spit in his face. You don't do that to a veteran who just came back from fighting against your kind. Not and live to tell about it."

"It was the only way," Roy agreed.

Forty-Three

Albert Sloan had learned just enough to get himself killed. Barlow had known what to expect that Friday afternoon, because Jerome Charlie had already been paid a visit, and he'd called Roy to tell him what the publisher was up to.

It was never clear what Sloan was up to. Jake told Helen that he didn't believe for a minute that Sloan intended to print a word about Growers Coast; he was merely trying to use the threat of publishing the story to shake down Barlow for a juicy long-term advertising contract. He also wanted Barlow's backing in the next mayoral election.

Sloan told Barlow in his office that day that he had written a "wicked three-parter" but felt uncomfortable about running it without some comment from "the ostensible founding family".

Barlow said he had to think about it and asked him to come back on Monday.

That evening, Barlow called Jake and told him they had a big problem. He said Sloan knew everything, and that meant, if it all came out, that the RCMP might question Barlow about Joseph Hara's death. "If they do, Jake, I can't promise to hide the truth," he said.

Jake thought he was joking at first. But Barlow said he was serious. He said if the whole story came out, he wasn't going to protect the Jacobsons and let the Barlow family name be linked to a possible murder.

"It was your dad, let's face it, who went crazy out there and killed the man," Barlow said.

Then Barlow asked Jake to "negotiate" with Sloan on his behalf.

Helen said Jake was hysterical at the thought that his dead father could be publicly identified as Hara's killer; it would mean ruination—certain defeat at the polls.

Friday evening, Jake called Sloan at his house, saying Barlow had asked Jake to check on the veracity of Sloan's information. Jake said he felt uncomfortable being involved —he was merely acting as a neutral party—but was willing to meet late that night and cover the bases with Sloan.

He took his unlicensed "regulator" with him, but later told Helen that he had no real intention of using it on Sloan, though he had an idea in the back of his mind about scaring the willies out of him.

Jake parked his truck on the shoulder of Beach Road near the Sloan house. He walked up the driveway and saw the light on in Albert's study, so he tapped lightly on the window.

Albert came to his door, speaking quietly so as not to wake Jan. He was very hyper. He said he wanted to *show* Jake exactly what had happened and would come out to his truck so they could take a short drive. Jake went back to the truck and waited. A couple of minutes later, Albert climbed into the passenger seat carrying his story and notes in a fat folder, along with a flashlight and rope with a noose tied at the end of it. When Jake looked at the noose, Albert snickered and raised his eyebrows like a stage villain. He said to drive out to Settlers Road first, and afterwards they could go to a Tim Hortons on the highway for coffee, and Jake could read the story. Jake glanced into the folder and saw the handwritten note to Barlow at the top of the cover page.

Jake drove to Settlers Road, listening to Albert tell him about Harry's photograph, the history of Growers Coast, the uprooting after the war and confiscation of property. Jake pretended he was flabbergasted by it all. Parked in front of the apple grove, Albert described Joseph Hara's grief at returning to find his family estate cut up and sold like chicken parts. He handed Jake his flashlight, walked over to the tree and pointed out the old moss-grown gash in the trunk, explaining how it got there. Then, with Jake providing the lighting, Albert flung the rope over one of the big main branches. Standing behind the fallen noose, he continued the story. "He hanged himself right here. They found him the next morning, but an amazing thing had happened. Somehow, this Japanese returnee had transformed overnight into a full-blooded Witka Indian."

Jake had heard enough, he later told Helen, and knew in a flash exactly what he was supposed to do. He aimed the pistol point-blank at Albert, told him to stick his head in the noose and tighten it, and the stunned publisher obliged. Jake took hold of the dangling rope end, heaved on it with both gloved hands until Albert was more than a foot off the ground, then lashed it from a lower branch to the trunk. It slipped a little in the tying but it held, and Albert strangled to death, just as Joseph Hara had fifty-five years before. "Only time I ever saw that pinko tongue-tied," Jake told a horrified Helen.

He was ready to drive away when he thought of the cover letter. He opened the folder that Albert had left on the passenger seat, read it again, and decided it would work in a pinch. He tore it off and stuffed it in Albert's coat pocket.

He later realized he had taken an insane risk; though Albert had assured him that Jan wasn't aware of the meeting, he fretted all night over the possibility that Albert had lied to him. He even thought at one point of going to the house and waking Jan, getting in there by saying something had happened to Albert, then shooting her. It would look like a murder-suicide. Luckily for Jan, by the time the idea came to him, he had drunk several glasses of rye and was too worried about being pulled over by the RCMP, then being linked to the night's mayhem, to carry out the plan. He also realized that too much time had passed; forensics would show that the suicide had come before the murder.

But the fear tormented him, and that was the reason he'd come to visit me the next day, figuring I was plugged into the *Chronicle* gang and would hear if his name had come up.

When he knew he could relax on that front, Jake then stepped up his fear campaign against the Shimizus, hoping to both silence them and drive them off the Coast. He made those prank calls on his cell phone, sitting in his car, tuned in to an aboriginal radio station that played West Coast spirit dance music for an hour every night starting at two a.m.

Then poor Jerome Charlie had made a fatal blunder. He called Jake Wednesday afternoon, about an hour after my visit—called him as a friend. He told Jake that he was convinced Barlow had been involved in Albert Sloan's death and was now afraid that he, Jerome, might be next. He said he was going to come clean about some ancient history that was a black mark against the Witka Nation. He wanted Jake's office to help set up a news conference for Friday, somewhere off the reserve. Jake believed the former chief's true aim was to "steal the rolling thunder" from Saturday's self-government signing ceremony—"a politician to the bitter end".

Jake told him to hold his water and wait till they could meet face to face. Jake said he personally wanted to keep out of the whole mess—"frankly it sounds dangerous, pardner"—but that they could meet up late that night on a bench they had often shared in the Witka cemetery and talk it over. He made Jerome swear that he wouldn't mention the meeting to anyone, not even his wife, because Jake needed to hear what the bad blood with Barlow was all about before committing himself to anything. Maybe after it was clear to him, he said, he would agree to stand by Jerome in public; possibly hold a joint press conference on Friday. Jerome said it was a non-issue: he had no intention of putting his wife in harm's way by telling her a thing about the Barlow matter.

That last precaution was obviously a lesson learned from the Jan Sloan scare; but again, Jake would later tell Helen that he didn't actually plan to kill Jerome Charlie. Sure, he packed his pistol to the meeting, but as an old friend, he thought he would be able to steer Jerome off his misguided course.

Jake parked his truck near the Harbour View Inn and stole along the beach to the reserve, hitting the cemetery just before twelve thirty, the appointed time. Jerome must have had qualms about the meeting, because he showed up packing his rifle under his arm. When Jake questioned him about it, acting shocked and hurt, Jerome said it wasn't a dig against him; Jerome believed Barlow had hirelings even on the reserve, just waiting for the word to take him out.

The two sat on the bench looking out to sea, which was almost blacked out under the starless sky. It was that night the clouds moved in, just before the rain. Jerome talked about the Ezra Paul deception, saying Barlow's old man had used it to cover up the death of a Japanese farmer who laid claim to some land at the other end of the peninsula. Jerome apparently wasn't too versed in the history. When Jake asked him how the farmer had died, Jerome said it was made to look like suicide, but his grandfather, Chief Benjamin, believed some of Barlow's thugs lynched the guy. Dick Barlow had asked the old chief for the name of a Witka family that had no living members left on the Coast, and Benjamin offered the Pauls as the first family that came to mind. In exchange for going along with the scheme, Benjamin secured title for the band to Crown properties on the east side of the highway—the area where the supermarket and behind it the gravel operation were now situated.

Jake said he did try to talk some sense into Jerome. He told him it would be pointless to go public with a yarn like that; there was nothing to be gained. It might give the Barlows a black eye, but it would make the ex-chief look silly and vindictive, killing his chances of ever returning to politics.

Jerome said he didn't care about how it would make him look. He was tired of sleeping with the lie. Besides, he said, he was pretty sure the Japanese farmer's family had returned to the Coast, and that's how Sloan had been tipped off. Now Pat Ross was digging into it. Better the band go public with it than be exposed as part of the dirty secret. Jerome said he knew he had to speak now, because he was having some awful dreams and believed spirits of the dead were angry with him for keeping the lie so long.

It was that "silly talk," Jake said, that made him realize there was no getting through to Jerome Charlie.

As they spoke, Jake had started pacing back and forth in front of the bench, feigning chill and slipping on his gloves. After a strong gust of wind he muttered, "That's going to fall," bent down and reached for Jerome's rifle propped up at the end of the bench, as if to move it. He checked to make sure it was ready to fire, swung it into Jerome's mouth and pulled the trigger.

Jake let the rifle drop on the ground and hiked back along the beach to his car.

The next day Roy Barlow phoned him and said Harry Shimizu had come by and laid his cards on the table. He also told Jake that he'd seen me sitting in my car in the parking lot and watched me follow Harry when he drove away. Jake drove up to Taylor Road, saw my car parked outside Sayonara Gardens, figured after about twenty minutes that I was getting the lowdown, then settled on his last plan for murder.

Forty-Four

Y ou were just lucky to have old Irving standing guard," Brennan said. "He had concerns about Jacobson from Friday on, after watching Jake burn Albert's papers in his fire pit in the middle of the night. He said his face"—Brennan put on Irving's plangent English accent—"was a *froitful* mask. A couple times during the week, after he saw Jake and you together, he considered warning you to watch the guy."

"Yeah, he told me when he was over here yesterday," I said. "But he said he didn't because I was a big city newspaperman, and he figured I'd be able to handle myself. It was the one thing Irving got wrong. But what's the deal with Helen Jacobson? How could she go along with Jake and his killing?"

"Both her and Jake have been on five different prescription drugs for quite some time, though it looks like Jake was off his meds for the past couple weeks. They've both been alcoholics for decades. I don't know how they did it. But they weren't well people. In fact, they were two very sick bunnies."

"I think I was picking up on it the last time I went over to visit them, the morning after Jake did in poor Jerome. I know I left there feeling not too well myself. But they still acted like a pretty normal couple."

"Maybe so, but it's all been confirmed by their shrink and their daughter in White Rock. Helen seemed to live almost exclusively through Jake—she quotes him all the time. Has she always done that?"

"Now that you mention it, yes."

"Jake put on a good front, but his shrink's been more worried about Jake than Helen for a dog's age. For Jake, the idea of losing political office had become life's big holy terror. When he got the first call from Barlow, he sat downstairs for an hour with that gun in his lap. Helen says she was petrified when he went out that night to meet Sloan, figuring he was going to drive into the bush and use the gun on himself. When he came back home, she was just so glad to see him alive that the things he told her were all very secondary. She didn't believe he killed Sloan. Same with Jerome Charlie. In both cases, what she thought happened was that Jake had come across their bodies, or heard about it on the radio, then imagined he'd killed them. Or was pretending that he had in some perverse attempt to impress her."

"Impress her?"

"Show that he could be as ruthless and decisive as his dad. She thought he was fantasizing at some level that he was his father—to keep his strength up. At least, that's what she claims. The woman's seriously ill. The deal the Crown cut with her lawyer was that if she told us everything she knew, and the family agreed to have her hospitalized, she wouldn't face charges. We didn't have a problem with that. We needed her full statement so we could build a case against Barlow."

"You're going after Barlow?"

"You bet. We'd like to see him charged with Sloan's murder and attempted murder against you. He played that sick bastard like a fiddle, and in both cases he put him up to it. Barlow's threat to expose Jake's father also led to Jerome Charlie's murder, but there wasn't the same direct involvement, so we're going to have to probably pass on that one."

"Does the Crown attorney think he can make a case?"

Brennan sneered. "They're already talking about bargaining

down to some kind of criminal negligence charges, if they have to. It all hinges on the quality of testimony Helen Jacobson can provide. She was standing right beside him when Jake got the calls from Barlow; hell, she listened to him the second time on the cordless, when Barlow was talking about you and Harry Shimizu. She says he told Jake he'd 'better get right on it.' Her recall is excellent, but her grasp of reality is the problem. She still doesn't believe Jake was capable of murdering anyone. Hopefully, the doctors can help her."

I walked him up to his car.

"That's a mean fried chicken and potato salad you do, buddy. Even got Ma Brennan beat, and that's saying a mouthful. You'll make some woman a good wife."

"Oh, they're looking for more than that in a man these days."

"We'll never be enough for them."

He climbed into his cruiser and buckled up. Then he clapped his John Law eyes on me. "Say, buddy, I figured you were owed one, so I gave you the whole shebang. But I will rely on your discretion. Know what I mean?"

I told him I did. "Come back next month for some pears."

"I might just," he said, looking down the slope. "Man, what a view."

I went back to the cabin and washed the dishes.

Forty-Five

Ifed the convoluted saga to Salim Marwari, who wrote up a murder main and a sidebar on the secret of Growers Coast that ran with Harry's photo. The main was chopped to ribbons after Barlow's lawyers put the fear of the mother of all lawsuits into the newspaper division's corporate brass. The Barlow name didn't appear in the final edit.

The story at least got it on the record that the recent deaths of two prominent Witka men were now being treated as homicides, and that the chief suspect, Conservative MP George Jacobson, had been killed by a citizen while attempting to murder a third victim, a former *Star* columnist who was investigating the mysterious deaths. The Mounties didn't confirm or deny any of it, and Irving stubbornly refused to be quoted or identified in the story, so I was the only named source, and virtually all the context I provided was chopped out. It was weak.

The Growers Coast sidebar caused little stir. It was one of those stories that people were pretty sure had been out there for a long time, only they'd missed it. Besides, the JCs had been compensated more than a decade ago; weren't the Ukrainians and Chinese the ones now seeking redress?

Neither story got picked up by other media, and both were widely dismissed on the Coast, since everyone knows that you can't believe anything you read in a tabloid.

The version that ran in the *Coast Chronicle* was even more oblique, because Barlow's army of lawyers had days instead of hours to shock and awe Jan's timid legal beagles, and Rita put up no resistance. In the end, only the murder angle made it into Coast homes; the Japanese connection was spiked entirely. If that wasn't bad enough, a wave of angry letters to the editor poured in calling the murder yarn itself nothing more than an outlandish fabrication, motivated by Jan's obvious personal stake in the matter and the *Chronicle*'s pathologically fixed bias against right-of-centre politicians. Since you can't libel a dead man, the readers fumed, poor George Jacobson was fair game. His former constituents, it turned out, thought the world of Jake; they just couldn't picture the folksy homegrown Member of Parliament for Witka embarking on a weeklong killing frenzy. So many chose not to.

I didn't bother telling Jan about Albert's supposed scheme to use his Growers Coast exposé as blackmail material. I wasn't sure I believed it anyway. He might have been testing and misdirecting Barlow, measuring how far his old enemy would go to keep the truth hidden before lowering the boom at the last minute, as he always had in his dealings with "the man". Of course, we would never know.

Barlow still hasn't been charged with anything. I don't ask Brennan about it. Just makes him angry.

Max Riverton pleaded guilty to the second-degree murder of Lars Lovedahl and got twenty-five years with no chance of parole for fifteen. And no, Joni Mitchell didn't write a song about him.

The moratorium on new salmon farms has been lifted, and there never was a report of a major vibriosis outbreak. The B.C. government, however, has started issuing health advisories warning consumers not to eat farmed salmon more than once a week.

Some descendants of the Japanese Canadian families

made it back for a roadside memorial service along the Coast Highway, near the presumed site of their old cemetery. It was darn sad seeing the elderly women standing out in the hot sun under their pink and orange parasols. The main group left on the next ferry.

I got to meet one of Joseph Hara's daughters. Kay was a jaunty, sweet little woman in her early seventies. She came out for the service and stayed on for a week with the Shimizus. One afternoon, Harry drove her down to my place, and we all sat around the living room munching on almonds and apples from one of the trees in the yard. Kay played me a round of cribbage and won every game. She didn't talk about her father or what had happened to him. At one point, she stopped shuffling the cards, looked out the window squinting, and said, "It's sure a beautiful view—I remember this view from childhood—and you've got a really great spot here, Pat. But it's the people that make the world or break it."

A few weeks after Kay left, the Shimizus moved back to southern Ontario. Ruby stuck to her parents.

Just after Christmas, the Mounties raided a fair size grow-op on Dolphin Inlet. The next morning before dawn, they executed a search warrant on a house on Lower Road and uncovered one of the biggest and most sophisticated grows in Coast history. They also seized almost half a kilo of cocaine, two hundred and twenty thousand dollars in cash, an arsenal of unregistered firearms, a handful of Taser stun guns, as well as paraphernalia and other evidence linking the home's occupant to organized crime on the Lower Mainland and the Island. With only a small possession fine from the seventies on his record, Big Bill was nevertheless sent to prison for eleven years. Of course, this is Canada, so he'll be out in just over four, but it's still heavy time. I used to feel regret and even moral indignation when I heard of growers getting sentences like that, but I was glad the judge gave it to Big Bill. I never did find the whip he said he planted in my house.

Sometimes I see Kewp in town, sitting by the window of a coffee shop on Cowrie Street, wearing one of her funky berets. A couple of happening dudes are usually sitting across from her. I always picture Big Bill there, too, scowling at the light. She motions for me to come over and join them, but I just wave back and keep walking.

CAST OF CHARACTERS

Pat Ross. Virgil Wood. Roy Barlow. George (Jake) and Helen Jacobson. Irving Walters. Tom Brennan. Pamela Grady (Kewp). Big Bill. Max Riverton. Jerome and Kate Charlie. Lars Lovedahl. Ian J. and Tish Cameron. Esther, Norman and Elijah Henry, and Louise. Albert and Jan Sloan. Harry and Ruby Shimizu. The old Scot. Joseph Hara. Dick Barlow. Benjamin Charlie. Salim Marwari. Rita Champion-Davis. Dennis. Reporters. Mounties. Mrs. Hutty. Sally. Marg. Superman and the Goon Squad. Gawkers. The faeries.

The characters, locale and incidents in this novel are entirely fictitious. Where actual historical events and figures do appear as background in the text, however, the author has made every effort to give truthful accounts, Joni Mitchell being a benign exception.

"What a Wonderful Wasted World" by John Gleeson originally appeared in the *Winnipeg Sun* on November 7, 2003.

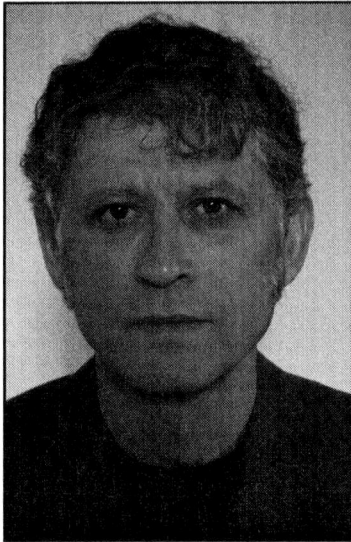

John Gleeson was born in Vancouver, British Columbia. He began his newspaper career at age sixteen, writing theatre reviews and covering news beats in the border city of White Rock. He shipped out as an ordinary seaman, clerked in a hardware store and failed as a gardener before returning to newspaper work.

An award-winning environmental reporter, Gleeson was city editor then editorial page editor for the *Winnipeg Sun* from 1997 to 2007. His writings have been reprinted in *The Week* and other U.S. publications. He has three grown children and currently lives and works in Winnipeg.